Time to Hit the Beach . . .

"Um, Mom," I said as I toyed with my scrambled eggs, "Joe and I would like to go down to the Jersey Shore for a week. Could we go?"

"By yourselves?" Aunt Trudy broke in.

She was sitting between us, looking from one of us to the other like we were out of our minds.

"I don't know, Frank," Mom said. "You boys just got back from a trip, and now you want to go away again so soon? Fenton, what do you think? Shouldn't they be spending more time at home?"

Dad lowered his newspaper—the one he likes to hide behind whenever there's a family dispute—and looked straight into my eyes.

I tried to signal him that this was important.

He seemed to get it. Turning to Mom, he said, "Well, dear, it is the summertime, after all. I think the boys are old enough to go to the beach on their own."

"Probably get themselves into more mischief," Aunt Trudy grumbled.

"It's true," Mom said, balling her napkin up into a knot. "Fenton, they only just got back—why do they have to leave again? Can't it wait till next week?"

I gave Dad another look. This couldn't wait.

THE HARDY BOYS
UNDERCOVER BROTHERS™

Available from Simon & Schuster

THE *HARDY BOYS*

UNDERCOVER BROTHERS™

#3   Boardwalk Bust

FRANKLIN W. DIXON

Aladdin Paperbacks
New York   London   Toronto   Sydney

♣ ALADDIN PAPERBACKS
An imprint of Simon & Schuster
Children's Publishing Division
1230 Avenue of the Americas
New York, NY 10020

THE HARDY BOYS MYSTERY STORIES and HARDY BOYS
UNDERCOVER BROTHERS are trademarks of Simon & Schuster, Inc.
ALADDIN PAPERBACKS and colophon are trademarks of
Simon & Schuster, Inc.
Designed by Lisa Vega
The text of this book was set in Aldine 401BT.
Manufactured in the United States of America
First Aladdin Paperbacks edition June 2005
10 9
Library of Congress Control Number: 2004116378
ISBN-13: 978-1-4169-0004-7
ISBN-10: 1-4169-0004-7

TABLE OF CONTENTS

Boardwalk Bust

1.

In Too Deep

Being buried alive is no fun. No fun at all.

Let me set the scene:

A waterfall of corn was raining down on me. The grains felt like millions of BBs as they bounced off my head.

A mountain of grain was rising like sand dunes all around me. It was at least ten feet deep. It had the consistency of quicksand. I was sunk into it almost up to my knees, and it was trying really hard to suck me down.

Meanwhile, the falling grain was sending up a billowing cloud of dust. I was totally choking on it.

Nice, huh?

It was mostly dark inside this grain bin, except for a distant square of light high above that threw faint shadows here and there. Corn was pouring through the hole—coming through the conveyor belt that a certain bad guy named Bill Pressman had started.

His intention? To kill me and Frank.

Why? That's a long story. But right now we were in trouble.

I could just make out my brother Frank. He was about twenty feet away from me, but it might as well have been twenty miles. He was well out of reach, and buried even deeper than I was.

"Joe!" I heard him yell over the roar. "Where are you?"

"Over h-here!" I shouted back, choking on the dust. "We've got to do something!"

"No, duh. Ya think?"

"Okay, genius," I said. "What's your brilliant plan?"

And, as usual, Frank had one. Over the years, I've come to count on his uncanny ability to pull impossible schemes right out of his ear.

"Joe, you've got to get out of here and shut off the conveyor!"

Uh, hel-lo. Anyone see me stuck in a pile of corn?

"I'm up to my knees in corn, bro," I said. "How am I supposed to do that?"

"Hey, I'm up to my chest! Just figure out a way—you've got to get over to that ladder . . . up there on the wall."

"Are you kidding me? I can hardly move—"

"J-Joe," he gasped, "I feel like I'm gonna be c-crushed if it gets much higher. . . . It's . . . gonna have to be you."

I could tell he wasn't joking now.

Desperately, I tried to wiggle free. I swung my body back and forth. When I had a little play, I shifted my weight to my right leg, which was on the low side of the corn pile, and twisted myself loose.

Then I rolled over, so I was lying with my back against the ever-shifting mountain. That way I could do things like breathe and see.

All right, so it wasn't so hard.

Meanwhile, the corn kept raining down, adding to the pile. The dust made it hard to see anything.

"Okay," I shouted. "Now what?"

"Shine your flashlight on me."

I pulled out my light wand—sort of a combination laser cutter and flashlight—and pointed it at him.

I could make out Frank now. He was holding up a pretty sweet gadget of his own.

"Use this grapple line," he said. "Catch!"

He tossed it to me. Luckily, I didn't miss it. It would have been buried under the corn for sure.

By this time I'd gotten Frank's intention. I aimed his gizmo at the ladder and fired.

The strong nylon line shot out and wound itself around one of the rungs of the wooden ladder. The hook at the end of the grapple dug into the wood.

I pressed another button on the handy-dandy contraption, and it reeled itself back in, drawing me forward. I was pulled up the slippery slope, gliding with ease. Before I knew it, I was on the ladder, climbing free of the death trap that still held my brother.

I kept climbing until I got to the door in the wall. The door was locked, of course—from the outside.

These guys thought of everything.

"I'll just use my laser cutter," I said, pocketing the grapple line and pulling out my other gadget.

"No!" Frank screamed. "Joe, grain dust is highly flammable—explosive, even! You'll blow us both to smithereens!"

"Hmmm," I said, stuffing it back in my pocket. "All righty, then. No lasers."

I tried brute strength instead.

Luckily, the lock was old and rusty, and it popped after five or six solid hits from my well-developed shoulder.

"Yes! Hang in there, Frank—I'll just be a second."

I scrambled down the ladder attached to the outside of the grain bin. As soon as I hit the ground, I hustled over to the switch that shuts off the conveyor belt. The machinery ground to a halt.

There.

I was surrounded by an eerie silence, broken only by the sound of my own heart pounding.

Luckily, Farmer Pressman seemed to be nowhere in sight. I realized with a sharp pang that he was probably gone for good, escaping justice in spite of all we'd done to catch him.

But there was no time to think about that now—I had to help Frank. I just hoped he was still breathing.

Along the side of the grain bin, I spotted a strange-looking yet familiar device. I recognized it from a newspaper article I'd read the week before. It was one of those new safety devices—what did they call it?

Oh yeah, a grain rescue tube!

But there was a complication. Between me and the rescue tube stood a cow. And not just any cow, but the cow that had kicked me in the eye just about an hour before.

Don't even ask. I was lucky it didn't blind me, and I'd be luckier still if I didn't have a black eye to show for it.

5

I yelled at the cow to move, but she didn't seem to get it. Cows are not the brightest.

Finally I lost my temper. I ran at the cow and shoved her out of the way.

"Moooo," she complained. But at least she didn't kick me this time.

I hooked the two halves of the rescue tube to the grapple line. Then I climbed to the top of the ladder, pushed the button on Frank's gizmo, and dragged them up after me.

Inside, the grain was no longer pouring off the conveyor belt. But Frank was now buried up to his neck, and I had to be careful coming near him.

One false move and I could have set off an avalanche, burying Frank in corn. Once I had the two halves of the rescue tube in place around him, I hammered down both sides with my fists, so that Frank was surrounded by a sort of plastic cocoon.

"Now start scooping out the grain," I told him.

"Can't," he gasped. "Can't move. Can barely . . . breathe. . . ."

I could see that the remaining grain inside the tube was squashing him pretty good. I realized I was the one who was going to have to get that corn out from around him and give him the space to haul himself out. So I hurried back outside, found a small shovel, took it back inside, and started digging him out.

Finally, after about fifteen minutes, Frank was able to wiggle himself up by the handles and get out. "I'm never eating popcorn again," he told me as we climbed the ladder out of there.

"No cornflakes for me."

"Corn muffins?"

"No way."

"I'm with you, bro."

We planted our feet on solid ground, and boy, did it ever feel good.

"No corn chips either."

"Okay," said Frank. "Glad we've got that straight. Now let's go get our bikes. We've still got a criminal to catch."

2.

Ride Like the Wind

We peeled out of there on our motorcycles, Joe and I, leaving a cloud of dust behind us.

We raced down the farm's driveway—really more like a long dirt road—zipping past the cornfields of Pressman Acres toward the main road.

The corn really was "as high as an elephant's eye," but Farmer Pressman, that no-good crooked slimebucket, was not going to be around to reap the benefits. That is, not if the sheriff had done his job and set up the roadblock like I told him to.

I couldn't really get a good breath till we were back on the asphalt of the main road again, tooling toward home.

About those bikes of ours. Just so you know, these are not just ordinary sport bikes. They've got

600 cc engines, huge twin caliper brakes, digital gauges, titanium-tipped exhaust pipes, twin front ram-air scoops—and that's just for starters. Add in a few nifty little trick gadgets straight out of James Bond, along with a whole lot of style—like the flaming double red Hs painted on the sides—shake well, and you've got yourself one *outstanding* ride!

I looked to my left at Joe and felt a rush of joy go through me. We'd almost been buried alive in that grain bin.

Breathing was good.

When Joe saw the flashers up ahead, he shot me a look—I could see the surprise on his face even under the visor.

I just nodded, trying not to be too much of a wise guy. But it was me, after all, who'd insisted on putting that phone call in to the sheriff—just in case we were walking into a death trap (which it turned out we were).

Joe had called me a wimp for bringing in the police. Now I was tempted to rub it in—but I controlled myself. If you're intelligent, like me, you don't bait people—especially when they're muscle-bound and temperamental, like Joe, and thus likely to knock you flat on your rear.

We slowed down as we passed. Three squad cars were blocking the road, and Pressman's huge

SUV was slung sideways in front of them.

There were skid marks where he'd hit the brakes. Soon there would be burn marks on his wrists, too. Those nylon handcuffs were chafing him as he sat with his back against a tree, trying unsuccessfully to work himself free.

Joe and I didn't stop to chat. We had been working undercover on this case. It wouldn't look good for the local sheriff—or for ATAC—if the newspapers found out that a couple of high school kids were involved.

This wasn't Bayport, after all. It was western New Jersey, and I doubt if they'd ever heard of Frank and Joe Hardy, "amateur teen detectives," around there.

It was just as well if the police took all the credit. ATAC is allergic to publicity. And as card-carrying members of ATAC—American Teens Against Crime—so are we. As we roared by the roadblock, Joe gave the sheriff a little salute. I didn't want to look like a jerk, so I saluted too. The sheriff smiled and waved.

Farmer Pressman saw the exchange, and it must have dawned on him who the guys under the visors were, because his eyes lit up like fireworks.

"Hey, you lousy kids!" he screamed.

The rest of what he said I couldn't hear. Sport

bike engines are really loud, especially when you gun them. I really didn't want to hear what he had to say, though, to tell you the truth. It wasn't going to be anything nice.

We left him to choke on our dust, and to meditate on the fact that crime doesn't pay.

I could tell Joe was laughing by the way his chest was bobbing up and down. It was funny *now*, sure— but I myself wasn't ready to start joking about it. We'd come pretty close to getting smothered.

Very uncool.

Pretty soon Joe stopped laughing. His eye was probably starting to hurt where that cow kicked it. Talk about *embarrassing*.

For the rest of the ride back to Bayport, we just concentrated on the highway and the wind in our faces.

Of course, at that point, we would have settled for a beat-up old Volvo. Anything was better than eating corn dust. It was good to be alive and on the way home.

We pulled into the driveway and parked behind Dad's old Crown Vic—the one he took with him when he retired from the police force.

It's an oldie but goodie, if you know what I mean. It's still got all the super-charged extras police cruisers have (and some others that they don't).

Dad was leaning against the fender with his legs and arms crossed and a sarcastic expression on his face. He'd been waiting for us.

"Well, nice of you two to show up. I was beginning to worry about you. What in the world happened?"

"We were reaping what we sowed," Joe said with a grin, shaking the last stray grains of corn out of his pants.

"Lucky you didn't meet the grim reaper," Dad answered. I could tell he was not amused. He stood up and started walking over to us as we put our kickstands down and our visors up.

"I just got a call from Chief Collig. He says the sheriff over in West Hoagland, New Jersey, reported the capture of a major drug smuggler."

Dad came up right between us and stopped. He crossed his arms again and continued, "This guy was a well-known local farmer, apparently. That factoid rang a bell. I remembered something about you two going off to visit a farm somewhere."

He looked at Joe, then at me. "Do you boys have something you want to tell me?"

Joe and I couldn't help grinning at one another. "Don't worry," I said. "We're untraceable."

"Nice work," Dad said, finally giving us a smile.

"Glad you're okay. Now go inside and get cleaned up. Your mom and Aunt Trudy have been waiting for you, and you look like something the cat dragged in."

Dad really does worry about us. It's not because he doesn't think we can handle ourselves in a tight spot. He knows we can.

It's just that he knows he's responsible for *everything*.

He's the one we took after, the one who taught us everything we know—up to a point. He's the one who inspired us to become amateur detectives years ago, when we were still little kids.

But most importantly, he's the one who founded ATAC and made us its first two agents. So like I say, it's not that he doesn't trust us—it's that he hates putting kids in harm's way. Especially his sons.

"Oh, and also," Dad added, "Trudy said something about sheets."

Sheets?

"Ugh," Joe said, putting a hand to his forehead. "I forgot—it's our day to help with the folding!"

Oh, right. Joe and I exchanged a quick look.

Our clothes were a mess, all ripped. I had scratches all over my arm from fending off Farmer Pressman's Dobermans. And Joe had the beginnings of a really magnificent black eye.

No way did we want to face Mom—and especially not Aunt Trudy—when we looked like we'd just been through a torture chamber.

Dad was staring at Joe's black eye now. He put a hand up to it. Joe flinched at the touch.

"What happened, son?"

Joe hesitated, so I just jumped in. "He got kicked by a cow."

"Shut up," Joe muttered, shooting me a look.

"A cow?"

"I . . . thought it would be a hoot to milk it," Joe said with a sigh. "You know, we were just hanging around in the barn, waiting for this scuzzball to show up . . ."

"Well, you'd better get in there and wash up before your mother and aunt see you like that," Dad said. "That way, you won't have to explain any of this."

We started for the kitchen door.

"And Joe—you might want to do something about that eye. You don't want to go telling people you got in a fight with a cow and lost."

"Dad's right," I said. "You might want to put some makeup on it."

Joe scowled at me. "Do I look like I would wear makeup?"

"Suit yourself," I said with a shrug.

14

We went into the house through the kitchen door. There are back stairs from there that lead up to our bedrooms—and, more importantly, the bathrooms.

We tiptoed our way along and were almost around the corner to the stairs when we heard Aunt Trudy's voice booming out from the living room. "Frank! Joe! I hear you clomping around in there!"

She came into the kitchen with Playback on her shoulder.

Playback is our pet parrot, and he loves to perch on Aunt Trudy's shoulder and nibble on her earlobe. It's probably because she lets him get away with it.

Aunt Trudy doesn't have any kids of her own, and she sure doesn't spoil us, either—but I'm telling you, as far as she's concerned, that parrot can do no wrong.

The funny thing is, when we first brought Playback home she hated him. She was totally grossed out by the way he pooped all over everything.

But one thing about our Aunt Trudy—she's a tough old bird. Tougher than Playback, anyway. Before too long, she had him toilet trained! No lie. That bird would not poop anywhere but in his cage, and from that time on, he was Aunt Trudy's baby.

"Got a good lie?" Joe whispered to me.

"I'll make one up."

"Oh, my goodness!" our mom gasped when she came into the kitchen and saw us.

"Holy mackerel!" Aunt Trudy nearly dropped the folded sheet she was holding.

Playback whistled long and low. "Aaawrk! Bad boys! Bad boys!"

"Joe! Your eye!" Mom said. "What in the world happened to you two? And no crazy made-up stories this time."

"Well," I began, "we kind of got caught in this grain bin . . . doing some research on farm safety devices . . ."

"Yeah!" Joe chimed in. "It's an over-the-summer school assignment!"

"Grain bin?" Aunt Trudy repeated. "Summer *assignment*? Ha! A likely story. They were probably at it again, Laura—chasing after another gang of crooks!"

"Now, Gertrude," our mom said, putting a calming hand out. "Don't condemn the boys before you check the evidence."

She went over to Joe and gently picked off a few grains of corn from his collar. "See? Corn. They're obviously telling the truth this time."

"Hmph," Aunt Trudy said. "Don't tell me. Evidence or no evidence, I know these two, and they've been up to no good."

"Crime-fighting isn't exactly being 'up to no good,' Aunt Trudy," Joe said.

Aunt Trudy raised one eyebrow, and Joe stopped right there.

"You'd better get yourselves cleaned up," she said. "These sheets will be all wrinkled by the time they get folded."

"Hop to it!" Playback squawked. "Hop to it!"

We ran up the stairs and got washed and changed as fast as we could, then came back down and started folding the sheets.

This has been a regular drill around our house since Joe and I were five years old. Every Saturday, Mom and Trudy wash the sheets, and Joe and I fold them. At this point we could do it in our sleep.

Still, Aunt Trudy never stops telling us how to do it just right. She's a laundry fanatic, coaching us like we're medical students doing our first brain surgery. Everything has to be done *exactly* her way.

"Pull on it—no, not like that . . . that's better. Left front corner over right rear, now right front over left rear . . . and make sure the corners match up!"

Et cetera.

After a half dozen or so sheets, we were just about done folding when the doorbell rang.

"I'll get it!" Joe said, eager to be the first one out of there.

Too late. I had already beaten him to it, dumping the sheet in his arms and heading for the front door.

"Hey!" I heard him shout behind me.

I opened the door—to find a Girl Scout, of all things.

"Hi!" she said, flashing me a big smile that showed off her very shiny metal braces. She had to be at least thirteen, maybe closer to fifteen. Kind of old for a Girl Scout . . .

"Wanna buy some cookies?"

She held out a box of Thin Mints.

"Um, no thanks," I said. "I think we've still got a few boxes from the last time. Hey, come to think of it, weren't you just here last month selling cookies? I thought it was a once-a-year kind of thing."

"Oh!" she said, her cheeks reddening. "Well, that was, um, another Girl Scout troop. Yeah, that's right. Our troop does it a month later." She laughed nervously.

"Oh, yeah? How come?"

"Um, just to be different?"

She shrugged her shoulders and giggled some more.

This was getting weird.

I had half a mind to say, "No, thanks" again and get it over with. We had enough Girl Scout cookies in the pantry. But this girl was pretty cute—even with her braces. And when cute girls smile at me, it always makes me nervous. I kind of choke up and, well . . . I start acting like a complete moron.

"Hmmm," I said. "How about some vanilla Trefoils?"

"Um, no," she said, shaking her head. "We're out of those. Try these Thin Mints instead."

Again, she thrust the box of cookies at me.

"No, really," I said, pushing them away. "I don't even like chocolate and mint together. It's . . . not my thing."

"Frank?" I heard Aunt Trudy calling. "Are you coming back in here? These sheets aren't going to fold themselves."

"Coming, Aunt Trudy!"

I turned back to the Girl Scout. "Look, I've gotta go," I said. "Sorry. Maybe next time."

"You dummy," she said, freezing me in mid-turn.

"Huh?"

"Just take them, okay?"

"I don't underst—"

Before I could finish, she shoved the dreaded box of Thin Mints into my hand.

"They're not cookies, doofus," she whispered, widening her eyes and staring at me.

"Not . . . cookies?"

"Nuh-uh."

"Ooooh. Okay, then," I said, getting it at last. "Sorry. I'm a little dense sometimes."

Especially around girls.

"Bye!" she said, giving me a wave and another big metal smile. "Good luck."

I opened the box, just to take a peek. Sure enough, there were no cookies inside. Instead there was a video game CD, with a label that read: BOARDWALK BUST.

Good luck?

Hmm. Maybe Joe and I were going to need it.

Turns out our cute little friend was no Girl Scout—she was from ATAC. And she had just brought us our next case.

3.

Shore Thing

I was in the living room, trying to do, by myself, what is impossible to do without someone else helping you: fold a queen-size fitted bedsheet.

And where was Frank? At the front door, talking to some girl.

I could hear them from the living room—when Playback wasn't screeching, that is. That parrot was busy using his feathers to mess up the sheets we'd already done. His idea of fun.

It's a strange thing about Frank and girls. They make him go all weird. He starts acting like a complete geek, which is not normally him. Well, maybe it is, just a little—but not as much as when girls are around.

Funny thing is, it seems to make the girls like Frank more than ever.

It gets me *crazy* sometimes. Frank can't dance, has no smooth moves, no dimple in his chin, no big muscles. All of which I've got in spades, by the way. But that doesn't seem to matter at all. Girls like Frank's bumbling shy act better.

I just don't get it.

Finally, Frank came back into the living room, and we started folding sheets again.

"What was that all about, dear?" Mom asked him.

"Girl Scouts," Frank said, looking at the floor. "Selling cookies."

"Well, I hope you didn't buy any," Aunt Trudy said. "Why, they were here just last month. I think it's nervy. How many cookies do they expect one household to buy?"

"Aaarrck!" Playback started in. "Get lost! Scram! Fuggedaboudit!"

"I didn't buy any," Frank said.

Then he noticed we were all staring at the box of Thin Mints sticking out of the back pocket of his cargo pants.

"Oh . . . these were a . . . uh . . . a free gift!"

"*Free gift?*" Aunt Trudy said, raising an eyebrow. "Well, now, that's different!" She smiled. "Frank, why don't you put them out on a platter and let's all have some?"

"Cookie! Cookie! Playback wanna cookie!" the parrot screeched, flapping his wings.

The panic in Frank's eyes was plainly visible, but he was looking at me. His back was to Trudy and Mom—and it was a good thing, too.

Obviously, he needed my help. I didn't know why, but I knew enough not to ask.

"Hey, Frank," I said, snapping my fingers. "Don't you and I have to finish that farm project for school? You know, write up the report?"

"For school?" Aunt Trudy said, raising her eyebrow so high it was halfway up her scalp. "It's *July*!"

"It's part of our summer project," I explained. "We have to do a blog. Daily entries. And we're way behind, aren't we, Frank?"

"Uh . . . yeah!"

"Hmmph." Clearly Aunt Trudy didn't buy it.

Lucky for us Mom was there. "Oh, let them go, Trudy," she said. "Can't you see they're tired of folding?"

"It's all that amateur detective nonsense," Trudy grumbled. "I don't know why you put up with it. If they were mine—"

"I know, dear," Mom said in the most soothing

voice you ever heard. "It's just *awful.* You boys are going to cut down on all that amateur sleuthing, aren't you? Promise me."

"Sure, Mom," we both said, crossing our fingers behind our backs. "You bet."

"All right, then, go on," she said. "We'll see you at dinner."

"Liar! Liar! Pants on fire!" Playback squawked as we ran up the back stairs to Frank's room.

That parrot is gonna get it one of these days, I swear. He's just lucky I'm a bird lover.

"Greetings, and welcome to Ocean Point, your very own paradise on the Jersey Shore!"

Frank and I sat glued to the computer monitor as the CD came on.

At first it looked like a typical travel advertisement aimed at potential tourists—except that it was computer animated, like any video game.

Our "host" was a voice-over, and the pictures showed a boardwalk crowded with happy beachgoers. There were people eating ice cream cones, cotton candy, and hot dogs. Little kids raced around in their bathing suits playing tag. In the background was the beach, with surfers riding the waves and swimmers bobbing up and down in the water.

Then the whole picture went to static. When it

came back into focus, we were staring at the face of Q.T., the director of ATAC.

"Hello, boys," he said, not smiling. (Q.T. never smiles.) *"Unfortunately, there seems to be a bit of trouble in this particular slice of paradise. Trouble in the form of a rash of burglaries."*

The monitor showed pictures of broken display cases, shattered plate glass, and bits of gold and silver scattered around everywhere.

"In the past month three jewelry stores in town have been broken into, causing heavy losses to the stores' owners. More serious, though, is the effect a crime wave could have on a beach resort like Ocean Point. The tourist season is just starting. You boys have got to stop these jewel thieves in their tracks before they scare the tourists away."

"Some time on the beach sounds good," I said to Frank, but he wasn't listening. When he's concentrating, nothing breaks through to him.

"In recent years, Ocean Point has become a haven for young people like yourselves," Q.T. went on. *"And since the local police seem to be stymied, I thought we'd put you two on the case. You'll find some spending money and one or two other things we thought might come in handy. Good luck—and you know where to reach me if you run into any trouble you can't get out of."*

"Yeah," I said, "how come we didn't try that when we were in the grain bin?"

25

"No cellular service," Frank reminded me, his eyes still glued to the monitor. "Dead zone."

Dead zone. Yeah, I'd say that grain bin was a dead zone, all right. We were lucky to have those gadgets on us.

"As you know, this CD will reformat to an ordinary music CD in five seconds. Your mission, as always, is and must remain top secret."

Frank and I silently counted to five. Sure enough, the picture went to a neutral background pattern, and music by the Surfaris started blaring out of the speakers. If Mom or Aunt Trudy had happened to open the door and peek in, everything would have looked normal—and that was the idea.

"Hmmm . . . jewel heists, eh?"

I reached into the cookie box and pulled out a nice-sized wad of cash. "Yes!" I said, starting to count it. "There's a good $500 here! You and I are gonna have a par-taaay on the beach!"

Frank gave me a smile and shook his head. "Born to be wild," he said, and shook out the rest of what was in the box.

There was a cheap disposable camera and a night vision telescope that collapsed down to the size of a shot glass.

"Hey, this is pretty cool," Frank said, playing with the scope.

Then he spotted the PDA. "Sweet!" he said, picking it up and turning it on. "Here we go. We've got all the names and addresses of the jewelry stores that have been hit, and some others that haven't been—yet."

He scrolled down and whistled. "Wow! Two hundred thousand dollars worth of stuff stolen from one store alone!"

"I've got a great idea," I said, hefting the wad of cash. "You and I could ride our bikes down there, but . . ."

"Yeesss?"

"Well, I don't know about you, but I'm starting to feel sore all over . . . and we'd be sitting in Sunday traffic for hours and hours. . . ."

"So . . . ?"

"Well, we've got enough money that we could *fly* down there," I suggested.

Oh, yeah—by the way, Joe and I are certified pilots, another one of the cool pluses of being ATAC agents.

"I don't know, Joe. That money has got to last us for who knows how long."

"Dude, how long could it possibly take to round up a gang of jewel thieves?" I said. "And anyway, the sooner we get there . . ."

"Okay." Frank gave in. "I guess you're right. I

am sore all over. Flying down will be relaxing."

"Exactly!" I said, slapping him—gently—on the back. "Now you're getting into the beach party spirit!"

"There's just one problem," Frank said, looking up at me.

"Yes?"

"How are we going to explain this to Mom and Aunt Trudy?"

I thought for a minute.

"Easy," I said. "We'll lie through our teeth."

4.

Lies, and the Lying Liars Who Tell Them

When Joe says, "We'll lie through our teeth," he means *I'll* lie through my teeth.

Joe's a terrible liar. I don't know if he's just too honest, or just a bad actor. All I can say is that somehow, whenever we have to fib our way out of—or into—a situation, it's always me who winds up doing the talking.

I've come to accept this. I used to fight it, but eventually I realized it was no use.

If we wanted our parents to let us fly down to the Jersey Shore for a few days of unsupervised "rest and relaxation," I was going to have to come up with a good line of baloney. No way could we risk revealing our true purpose.

There's a very good reason why ATAC is top

secret, see. If bad guys knew about it, they might try to get even with us agents—or even our families. On the other hand, you can't get information out of someone who doesn't know anything. So the fewer people who are in on the secret, the better.

Not that Mom and Aunt Trudy don't get suspicious sometimes.

It goes back to the days when Joe and I were kids, solving cases we weren't supposed to even get involved with. We got pretty well known there for a while, but ever since Dad created ATAC, we've tried to keep our activities quiet.

That means a whole lot of lying to everyone we know, except Dad. I don't like it, and neither does Joe, but it's the price we have to pay if we want to fight crime in a big way.

So the next morning I had my bag of lies all ready to go.

"Um, Mom," I said as I toyed with my scrambled eggs, "Joe and I would like to go down to the Jersey Shore for a week. Could we go?"

"By yourselves?" Aunt Trudy broke in.

She was sitting between us, looking from one of us to the other like we were out of our minds.

"I don't know, Frank," Mom said. "You boys just got back from a trip, and now you want to go away again so soon? Fenton, what do you think?

Shouldn't they be spending more time at home?"

Dad lowered his newspaper—the one he likes to hide behind whenever there's a family dispute—and looked straight into my eyes.

I tried to signal him that this was important.

He seemed to get it. Turning to Mom, he said, "Well, dear, it is the summertime, after all. I think the boys are old enough to go to the beach on their own."

"Probably get themselves into more mischief," Aunt Trudy grumbled.

Aunt Trudy loves us, but she's always afraid we're going to get hurt. And I guess she has reason to be nervous. Joe and I have gotten into more dangerous situations as kids than most people do in their whole lives. "And how are they going to get there?" she continued. "Not on those motorcycles, I hope! Do you know how dangerous those things are? And look at the way they looked last night!"

"It's true," Mom said, balling her napkin up into a knot. "Fenton, they only just got back—why do they have to leave again? Can't it wait till next week?"

I gave Dad another look. This couldn't wait.

He cleared his throat. "Um, actually, I've got the wood for the new backyard fence being delivered next week. I was hoping the boys could help me with that. This week would be better."

"Well," Mom said, turning to me and Joe, "I hope at least you won't take your motorcycles this time. I'd feel better if you gave them a rest for a while."

"We won't, Mom," I promised. "Right, Joe?"

"Nope," he said, giving her a smile and crossing his heart.

"They still have buses that go down there from the city, don't they?" Mom asked.

"Um, actually," I said, "we thought we might fly down."

I'd been saving this information till we got permission to go. Now I sprung it on them, knowing full well how they'd react.

"Are you *serious*?" Aunt Trudy said.

"What? We're licensed pilots," Joe pointed out.

"Yes," Trudy agreed. "But that doesn't make you *good* ones."

"Now, Trudy," Dad said, "I've flown with the boys, and they're both perfectly fine pilots."

"Then why is it that every time they fly, something terrible happens?" Trudy asked.

"Mayday! Mayday!" Playback screeched, flapping his wings. "SOS! We're going down! Mayday! Mayday!"

"Shhh!" Trudy silenced him, giving him a cornflake. "Last time they flew a plane, as I recall, there was engine trouble—or at least that's what the story was."

"It *was* engine trouble, Aunt Trudy," Joe said.

"Really? Well, it just so happens Adam Franklin is an old friend of mine. He swore up and down that he'd looked over that engine six ways from Sunday before you boys took the plane up."

Joe and I exchanged a glance. We knew we were caught in a lie. That plane hadn't had engine trouble—it literally had a monkey wrench thrown into it. And it wasn't Adam Franklin, our trusty airplane maintenance man, who'd thrown it.

"And then there was the time before that. What was it, a mysterious hole in the gas tank?"

"Look, it's probably just a run of bad luck," said good old Mom. "I know my boys, Trudy, and they're certainly not reckless pilots."

"So it's settled then?" I jumped in, before anyone could say anything else about our flying skills.

"Just be careful," our dad said, putting a merciful end to the discussion. "You boys have enough money for your trip?"

I thought of the cash that had come in the cookie box. I also knew that, thanks to ATAC, the flight down to Ocean Point would be covered separately.

"We'll be fine," I said.

"All right, then," Mom said. "When do you mean to go?"

"Right after breakfast," I told her.

Joe had already shoveled his breakfast down his gullet. I now followed suit, and we got out of there. We had a mission to start, and I didn't want to have to tell any more lies—at least not to our family.

As we left the kitchen, I heard Playback serenading us, displaying his usual sense of humor.

"Mayday! Mayday! We're goin' down, boys! SOS!"

"You sure she's fit to fly?" I asked Adam Franklin as we climbed aboard our two-passenger Piper—Joe at the controls, me sitting behind him to navigate. We'd called about an hour ahead so he could get our plane ready.

"Oh, you bet!" Adam said, taking off his Red Sox cap and scratching his bald head. "Last time your Aunt Trudy gave me what for about it!"

"Hey, that's ancient history," I said. "Don't worry about it, Adam. Let's focus on this time."

"No prob," he said, giving us a wave and patting the silver side of the plane. "She's in perfect shape. Weather's good too. You boys have a nice flight. Take my word for it, it'll be a safe one—long as you don't do any loop-de-loops."

Soon we were airborne and headed south.

We picked up the Jersey Shore at Sandy Hook and kept it in sight as we went. We passed over Long Branch, Monmouth University, and the Shark River Inlet.

It was right about when we hit Long Beach Island that the fog bank rolled in from out of nowhere.

Within the space of two minutes, we were flying totally blind, relying only on our dashboard compass for direction. These little one-engine jobs don't have radar, in case you were wondering. You're basically not supposed to fly them in bad weather.

"Where did this stuff come from?" Joe asked, frowning at the fog. "I thought Adam said the weather was going to be fine."

"You know Jersey. If you don't like the weather, wait a minute."

"I know our luck with airplanes," Joe replied. "And so does Aunt Trudy."

"Just keep us headed the right way," I told him. "This can't last long."

Mmm hmm. Famous last words.

The fog lasted for a good ten minutes. And when we finally came out of it, there was another plane coming right at us.

5.

Beach Bound

"Bank left!"

I didn't need Frank screaming in my ear to know what to do. In that moment I was all instinct. I pulled on the throttle and my stomach turned as we banked hard left—so hard that we were upside down for a moment before we came back around.

"Whew!" I said. "That was close!"

"Too close," Frank agreed. I could feel him grabbing my leather jacket for all he was worth. He was holding on so tightly that I couldn't move to maneuver the plane.

"Dude, let go of me," I said. "I've gotta fly this thing."

He let go, but the plane kept bucking. "What's going on?" I asked.

36

Frank looked behind us, then yelled, "There's something caught on our tail!"

Just for a second, I risked letting go of the controls to get a look.

Sure enough, there was a big piece of cloth caught on our tail. It was flapping wildly in the wind, dragging the back of the plane down. If we didn't get it off, and quick, it was going to make us stall out.

Not good.

Neither of us needed to say anything. We both knew we had only one option—one of us had to climb out onto the fuselage and pull the cloth free, or we were going to take a fatal dive into the Atlantic Ocean.

"I'll go," I said.

"No! You stay put—just try and keep us steady."

Before I could argue with him, Frank pulled back the cockpit cover and climbed up and out, onto the top of the fuselage.

I couldn't bear to watch, and anyway, I had to keep the plane sure and steady so he didn't fall off. We were a good thousand feet up, and as good a high diver as Frank is, there was no way he could have survived a plunge like that.

I happen to be a crackerjack pilot, but this plane was getting almost impossible to control. (*You* try keeping a small airplane steady with someone climbing on it!) The closer Frank got to the tail, the more he was throwing off the plane's balance, and the harder my job was getting.

I felt a sudden easing of the drag, and a minute later Frank tumbled back into his seat behind me. "Whew!" he said. "That was exciting."

"What in the world was that thing?"

"One of those banners—you know, the ads planes fly back and forth over the beach?"

"You're kidding," I said. "That plane that almost hit us . . ."

Now it was clear what must have happened. We'd avoided hitting the plane, but the banner it was trailing got snagged on our tail. We were just lucky it had snapped off the other plane, or it could have dragged both aircraft down.

"It took a little chunk out of our tail," Frank told me. "How's she flying?"

"Not too bad," I said, "but we'd better take her down before we lose anything else."

"Where are we?"

I looked around and saw the familiar shapes of Atlantic City's many casinos in the distance. "There you go."

"Atlantic City? But that's forty miles from—"

"I know, dude," I said. "We'll just have to get

there some other way. I'm not risking it. We've had enough excitement for one flight."

He didn't argue. I guess we were both a little shell-shocked. First the grain bin and now this—and all in the space of twenty-four hours!

We finally landed at the Atlantic City airport and phoned Adam to let him know what had happened. Adam's in on the ATAC secret, luckily. He said not to worry about it, that he'd take care of it with a few phone calls.

Now the only problem was how we'd get to Ocean Point. We're not old enough to rent a car, and our bikes were back in Bayport. Being stranded in Atlantic City with a bunch of cash may be some people's idea of a good time, but we had a mission to accomplish in Ocean Point, and no way to get there.

"How 'bout a taxi?" Frank suggested. He pointed to a row of cabs parked outside the terminal building.

"No way," I said. "Ocean Point is forty miles from here. Do you know how much that would run us? We'd be blowing a big chunk of our budget before we even got there! And I am primed for some serious spending."

Just then I felt somebody tapping me on the shoulder.

"Excuse me, son," a deep, booming voice said. "Did you say you needed a lift to Ocean Point?"

I turned around and took a good look at this human megaphone. He was a big, brawny guy—I guessed about fifty years old, six feet, maybe 230 pounds, with a bushy head of brown hair that was getting gray around the temples.

This guy looked like he spent most of his time out in the sun. His tanned face brought out the whiteness of his big teeth when he smiled. The smile looked like a professional dental job—a really expensive one.

"Yes, sir," Frank said. "We were headed there in our plane, but we had a little trouble with it."

"Oh yeah? What sort of trouble?"

I told him about our near miss. He shook his head and frowned.

"Mmmm, yeah. Some of those banner pilots are real cowboys," he said. "You boys are real lucky to be alive."

"You can say that again," I said.

"Name's Bump," he said, holding out his hand. "Bump Rankowski."

I shook it, and he nearly crushed my hand in his grip. *Whoa.* This guy was strong. "Joe Hardy," I said. "And this is my brother Frank."

"Good to meet you, Frank," Bump said, crushing Frank's hand in turn.

I flexed my own, just to make sure it wasn't broken.

"So you say you're headed to Ocean Point? Well, that's where I'm headed too—just got clearance from the tower. Would you like a lift? No charge."

To tell you the truth, getting back in a plane just then was the last thing I wanted to do, and I'm sure Frank felt the same. On top of that, we didn't know this guy from a hole in the ground, and who could tell what kind of pilot he was?

On the other hand, if he *wasn't* a terrific pilot, either of us was plenty good enough to help him correct a mistake or get out of a jam.

Besides, what better choice did we have? Opportunity was knocking, and we weren't about to let a lucky break go by.

"Excellent!" Frank said.

"Sweet," I agreed. "You're sure it's not—?"

"No problem," Bump said. "I've got me a four-seater. Unless you've got company, I count three of us. You ready to fly?"

He gave us another dazzling smile and put a powerful arm around each of our shoulders. "Come on—she's parked right outside."

"This is really great of you, Mr. Rankowski," Frank said.

"Please, call me Bump. Nobody calls me by my last name. Not once we've shook hands."

"If you don't mind my asking, "Frank said, "how did you get—"

"The name Bump?" he finished, laughing. "*That's* how—check her out, boys. She's good for a bump or two, all right!"

Removing his arms from around our shoulders, he pointed to a Day-Glo red Cessna parked across the runway. The teeth and eyes of a great white shark were painted on the sides.

"Awesome!" I said, going over to take a closer look. "Oh, man! This thing rocks!"

"Meet Jaws. She's my pride and joy," Bump said, patting the side of the plane. "Go on, hop in."

"Whoa," Frank said, admiring the instrument panel. It was all sporty; all the dials were phosphor white.

We got strapped in while Bump started going through his preflight checklist. "My birth name was Arnold," he said, "but I never liked it. So when people started calling me Bump, I let 'em."

He started the engine. "So, what brings you boys to Ocean Point? Little vacation?"

Frank gave me a look of caution—like I didn't know to watch what I said. I mean, give me a break! "Fourth of July weekend," I said. "Gotta hit the beach, right?"

"You bet!" Bump said. "You look like you could use a break, Joe. Get punched in the eye, did you?"

"Um, sort of."

"Kicked, actually," Frank volunteered.

I kicked him in the ankle to keep him from saying anything else about it. "It's a long story," he said, wisely leaving it at that.

"Well, anyway, you can't find a better beach than Ocean Point. Best spot on the whole Jersey Shore—and I oughta know. After all, I'm the mayor."

"The mayor?" Frank said, sitting bolt upright in his seat. "Wow!"

"Yup, that's me—live and in person."

Bump gunned the engine, and we started taxiing down the runway. The noise was deafening, but Bump had the kind of voice that can cut through anything—a politician's voice. "Lived in Ocean Point all my life. You want to know something about the place, I'm the guy to ask."

Frank and I exchanged a quick look. This was a perfect chance to start our investigation—but we had to be careful. Bump Rankowski seemed like a friendly guy, all right, but as the mayor of a town with a crime wave, he might be sensitive to certain kinds of questions.

We sat back and waited till Bump got us airborne. He did a slow turn, and we headed back north, keeping the shoreline on our left. There was no trace of the fog bank that had nearly killed us.

"Boy, the weather sure changes fast around here," Frank said.

"You got that right," Bump said. "Gotta keep your eyes open when you're flyin' the beach."

"Flying the beach?" I repeated.

"I'm a banner pilot too," Bump said. "I own a six-plane outfit. You see a banner being flown this week, it's probably me or one of my boys." He pointed to a big white button above his head. "See that? That unfurls the banner."

"You own the company?" I asked.

"That's what pays for things like this baby." He patted the ultra-high-tech dashboard with its expensive wood and gold trim.

I thought of the pilot who'd nearly killed us less than an hour ago. "You weren't up flying today, were you?" I asked.

"Naw, not with the fog," he said. "I grounded my entire fleet at four o'clock when we got the forecast. . . . Oh, I get what you're thinkin'! No, it wasn't me, or any of mine. Ha! That's funny!" He laughed hard, slapping his knees.

It wasn't *that* funny.

"Are there other companies that fly the beaches?" Frank asked.

"Oh, yeah. There are three or four outfits that run advertising up and down the shore. Some of 'em will hire any old pilot too—sounds like you boys ran into a real cowboy."

"I don't think he saw us coming, any more than we saw him," Frank said.

Bump shook his head in disgust. "He shouldn't even have been up there. Once fog rolls in, it's way too dangerous—well, I guess I don't have to tell you that!" He laughed again. "Listen, I'll try to find out who it was. Can't let him get away with shenanigans like that."

I hated to see somebody get fired, especially since there was no way it was intentional. "Aw, that's okay," I said. "I think we'd rather just let it go. . . ."

"Now, you just leave it to me," Bump said, turning back to look at us. "It's my job to keep my town safe, and that's what I'm gonna do." He nodded slowly. "I know people, and I can get things done. You just watch me."

There was something about the way he said it

that gave me a chill. Underneath his friendly politician act, I could see that Bump Rankowski wasn't somebody you'd want to cross.

The sun was setting, and lights were coming on all along the shore. "There's Ocean Point now!" Bump said, pointing to a cluster of lights in the distance. "Beautiful, isn't she?"

We nodded in agreement, staring down at the town as we approached. I could see a boardwalk with lots of stores, restaurants, and attractions. There was even a small pier with rides and arcades—sort of a miniature version of Seaside Heights or Asbury Park.

"Looks like a good time," I said, giving Bump a wink.

"Oh, you boys are gonna flip for it," he assured us. "No place like it."

Frank cleared his throat, and I knew what was coming. "Um, didn't I read something somewhere about some robberies happening there recently? What was it, jewelry stores?"

I could see Bump's face freeze into a mask. His smile was still in place, white as ever, but his eyes had changed somehow. Behind them, the wheels were working.

"Oh, that," he said, forcing a laugh. "Just a once-in-a-blue-moon kind of thing. You know, people come into town from all over. Once in a while, there's bound to be a bad apple."

"Right," Frank agreed, but I could tell he was starting to get suspicious.

<u>SUSPECT PROFILE</u>

<u>Name:</u> Arnold "Bump" Rankowski

<u>Hometown:</u> Ocean Point, New Jersey

<u>Physical description:</u> Age 48, 6', 230 lbs., ruddy complexion, deep suntan, graying hair, always smiling, big teeth.

<u>Occupation:</u> Mayor of Ocean Point

<u>Background:</u> Wealthy entrepreneur/politician who was born in Ocean Point and wound up as its mayor. Never married. No children.

<u>Suspicious behavior:</u> The sense that he's got a secret.

<u>Suspected of:</u> Is he hiding what he knows about the jewel thefts?

<u>Possible motives:</u> Saving his town's reputation, maybe?

"Has the thief been caught yet?" Frank asked.

"Not yet," Bump said, staring straight ahead as he pointed us toward the landing strip. "But we've got the best police department on the whole shore, and they're on the case. Don't you boys worry. Ocean Point is as safe a spot as you'll ever find."

He brought us in for a perfect landing, and we taxied to a stop outside the small terminal building. "Come on," he said. "I'll drive you to your hotel. Where are you staying?"

"Well, we hadn't figured that out yet," I said. "Any suggestions?"

"Are you kidding?" he said. "I've got a million of them."

He drove us to the Surfside Inn, just half a block from the boardwalk. "Here you go," he said, pulling over. "Best spot in town if you're on a budget—and most kids your age are."

"Thanks, Mr. Rankowski," Frank said. "I mean, Bump."

"Don't be strangers, now. If you need anything, you can find me at City Hall, over on Main Street."

"Well," Frank said, as Bump pulled away in his big black Lincoln. "That was interesting."

"Weird," I said. "What did you think of our new friend?"

"He's definitely a politician," Frank said. "You've

got to take everything he says with a grain of salt."

"Did you see how he froze up when you mentioned the robberies?"

"Definitely."

"I guess he's not happy that the news is getting around."

"Would you be, if you were the mayor?"

"Good point," I said. "Well, I don't know about you, but I'm beat. Let's check in, get some supper, and hit the sack."

"What, no partying?" Frank said, giving me an elbow in the ribs.

"Shut up," I said.

6.

Ocean Point

I woke up the next morning when the sun rose over the horizon and shone right smack into my face. It glinted over the ocean, magnifying the light till it was blinding. There was no way to keep on sleeping.

"Oh, man," I said to Joe, who was holding his pillow over his head to keep the light away. "You forgot to close the curtains!"

"*I* forgot?" He threw his pillow at me. I threw mine at him.

"Close the curtains," he said.

"Me? Why me? You're closer to the window."

"Because, dude," Joe groaned. "I hurt all over."

"*You* hurt? Hey, I'm the one who almost got crushed in that grain bin!"

"Big deal," Joe said. "I'm the one who got kicked by a cow!"

"I'm the one who went out on the wing of the plane!"

"Okay, okay," Joe said, hoisting himself up and going to close the curtains. Half a minute later he was back in bed and passed out.

Despite my victory, I couldn't get back to sleep, so I took a hot shower instead. It took some of the soreness out of my muscles. Then I went downstairs to check out the scene.

It was a gorgeous summer morning. The hotel was only half a block from the boardwalk. In between was a miniature golf course, already packed with kids and their parents.

It was a little early for swimming, but by ten o'clock, lots of people would be on the beach and in the water. It was going to be a hot one.

I had some pancakes at the restaurant up the block, then went back up to the room to wake Joe. Time was a-wasting. We had to get started if we wanted to nail our serial jewel thief.

Joe was already up, out of the shower, and in his bathing suit. "Time to check out the scenery!" he said. "I'm feeling ir-res-istible today. Hey, how does my eye look?"

"Better," I lied. "It barely shows. Still, you'd better

come up with a good story to explain how you got it."

"Whatever I do come up with, you'd better back me up."

"Don't worry about it."

"Come on, let's hit the beach."

"Joe, don't you think we'd better do some investigating first? I mean, we're here on a case, remember?"

Joe gave me a look. "All work and no play makes Frank a dull boy."

"How 'bout we go to the jewelry stores that got hit, and see what we can find out?" I suggested.

"Later," Joe said, admiring himself in his new bathing suit. "Gotta take a swim first."

"Joe . . ."

"Maybe do a little surfing . . . we could rent boards. . . ."

"Joe . . ."

"Hey, there's information to be dug up on the beach, too, right? Right?"

I sighed, shook my head, and went to get my suit on.

There's no arguing with Joe sometimes. Like when the surf looked this good.

Hang on, I've got to step in.

In his heart Frank *knew* I was right. There was no better way to get the lay of the land than to go out and do what everyone else was doing.

In Ocean Point that meant swimming. It meant surfing. It meant beach volleyball, cruising the boardwalk, hitting the arcades and amusement park rides, finding cool junk and funky T-shirts in the gift shops and stores. It meant checking out the sidewalk artists and performers who were everywhere in this honky-tonk beach town.

And ah, yes, taking in the bikini parade. *Awesome.*

It meant eating at pizza joints and soft ice cream stands, hot dogs and pretzels and cotton candy . . .

Suddenly I realized I hadn't eaten breakfast. "Frank," I said. "Let's stop and get something to eat."

"No thanks," he said. "I already ate."

"Huh? When was that?"

"While you were sleeping."

Frank can be so annoying sometimes.

"You didn't bring me anything back?"

"I didn't know what you'd want."

Yeah, right. "Okay, well, I've gotta eat something. *Now.*"

"Whatever," he said.

We went outside and headed for the boardwalk. Right away I spotted a sign that read: SALTWATER TAFFY—HOMEMADE!

Sounded good to me. I always like to sample the native cuisine. We started heading over.

Over at the amusement park on the nearby pier, we saw some kids screaming on the Ferris wheel. There was a tattoo parlor called Rat-a-Tattoo, and a sign that read: FREAK SHOW—TICKETS $10!

As we entered the saltwater taffy place, we saw this guy behind the counter who—I swear— looked like he was *made* out of saltwater taffy. He was fat, and flabby, and bald, and slightly green. He was reading the morning paper.

"Hi, I'd like some taffy," I told him.

He lowered his paper and slid off his stool. "What flavor you want?" he asked. He had an accent—Russian, it sounded like.

"I don't know . . . the pink," I said.

"Strawberry . . . good choice. How much you want?"

"I don't know," I said. "Enough for breakfast."

He didn't bat an eyelash.

With a big, scary-looking knife, he sliced off a

piece of the sticky stuff, slipped it into a plastic bag, and handed it to me. "Six-fifty," he said.

While I was fishing out my wallet, Frank asked him, "Is there really salt water in saltwater taffy?"

The guy smiled. His teeth were all rotted out and black, naturally.

"Nah!" he said. "Good question, though. Most people assume it's made out of salt water. Americans, they aren't very curious. You're a smart boychick."

"Smart what?" Frank said.

"Boychick. Russian for boy. So *you* want some taffy too?"

"No, thanks," Frank said. "My brother's the one with the sweet tooth."

"Smart kid," the man said, chuckling. "Thinks about his teeth, they shouldn't get cavities."

He turned to me. "You should be more like your brother. Maybe then you won't get black eye."

"How do they make taffy?" Frank asked him, before I could tell the guy where to get off.

"*They? I* make it! Right here in the store."

He pointed to a big machine in the back of the shop that was churning a load of gooey green taffy in spirals, over and over and over again. "That's how we do it. Gotta spin for four hours to get the right softness. You buy it in supermarket, it's not the same thing."

"I bet it isn't," Frank said, looking at the man's newspaper. "So, what's all this about robberies in town? Any idea who's behind it?" Frank asked, pointing at the front page.

Now I saw why he'd been wasting his time on this slob. Frank never stops thinking.

"If you ask me, everybody here has racket. This is just the same thing, only big-time. Everybody is con artist."

I bit my lip. What were Frank and I, if not con artists? Making people believe we were just here for a little fun in the sun, while all the time we were really tracking down a brazen thief?

While they were talking, I was trying to break off a piece of taffy to start chewing on. It didn't want to stop stretching, though, and pretty soon I was fighting with it, backing up toward the window.

Suddenly something grabbed me by the hair.

"Aaargh!"

"NO!" the taffy man shouted. "Don't go there! You'll get stuck!"

"Thanks for the warning," I said, holding onto the hair that was now stuck to one of the big wads of fresh taffy hanging in the shop window. "A little late, but much appreciated. Could you please help me get free of this?"

Frank came right over, but the guy just stood

there shaking his head. "You not gonna get it off like that," he said.

He came toward us with his big knife. Before I could stop him, he cut me loose from the hanging taffy. Now there was just a small piece of it stuck to my hair.

"Don't pull on it, or your hair's gonna come right out," he told me.

"Well, how am I supposed to get this off of me?"

"Joe, don't panic," Frank told me.

"What do you mean, don't panic?"

"Salt water," the guy said.

"What?"

"With salt water, will come right off. You'll go in the ocean, bim-boom, it comes right off you hair."

"Whew. What a relief," I said, backing out the door. "Well, bye. Nice talking to you. Come on, Frank—I've gotta get this off right *now.*"

We crossed the boardwalk and went down the wooden stairs to the beach. There we were, surrounded by kite flyers, Frisbee flippers, volleyball players, and boogie boarders. Everywhere we looked, there were blankets spread out, with cute girls busy getting tans.

"Hi!" one of them said as we passed.

For a fatal moment, I forgot what was attached to my hair.

"Hi yourself," I said, putting on my smoothest move. "What's up? Looking for some company?"

She giggled, and now both she and her friend were checking us out. I sat down next to the one who'd said hi.

I could tell Frank wanted to get on with our job here, but he saw that I was determined not to be rude to our fine new friends, so he sat down too.

Within ten seconds the two girls were surrounding Frank—as far from me on the blanket as it was possible to be. "What is that thing in his *hair*?" I heard one of them whisper in Frank's ear.

"And what happened to his eye?" the other one asked, looking at me.

"Um, it's a long story," I said, standing up before they could see how red my face was getting. "Frank will tell you all about it. I've gotta go cool off in the water. . . ."

I ran for the ocean as fast as I could.

What a doofus! How could I have forgotten how geeky I looked with that taffy sticking up from my hair?

Later, I promised myself, I'd go back to that store and get my money back.

The water was cold when I dove into it, but after ten seconds of screaming, I started to get used to it. Then I got busy scrubbing the stupid taffy off.

Lucky for that guy, he wasn't kidding. The taffy came right out.

Too bad I still had that black eye. Frank was right—I should have gotten some makeup for it.

I came out of the water, feeling embarrassed but ready to get on with my life. I saw that the two girls both had their arms around Frank and were laughing their heads off. Frank looked like the cat that ate the canary.

I was about to go over there and remind him that we were supposed to be fighting crime when I noticed something I'd never seen before. It was a huge drawing in the sand, probably created with rakes. Very cool.

I looked at it more closely and saw that it was really an advertisement. THE SHORE THING: FINE JEWELRY, it read.

There was a guy with a metal detector walking across the beach, slowly waving it back and forth. He was about to step right on the embossed ad— on the Y in Jewelry, to be exact.

"Hey!" I called out to him. "Watch where you're walking!"

He stopped and looked up at me with a face that would freeze a furnace.

This was perhaps the ugliest dude I'd ever seen. And his expression was even uglier. He kept staring at me as he marched forward, stomping right through the artwork.

I made a mental note to tell Frank about him. A mental note that I immediately proceeded to forget.

"Come on, lover boy," I told Frank when I reached the little threesome. "We've got work to do."

"Sorry," Frank said to the girls as he rose. "Joe's right. We do have to go."

"Aw, what's your hurry?" the taller of the two girls said.

"Wait a second," said the other. Whipping out a pen from her beach bag, she wrote her phone number on Frank's palm. "See you soon?"

"S-sure," Frank said.

I pulled him away before he could say anything to embarrass himself.

We were about to hit the boardwalk, looking for the first of the jewelry stores on our list, when we heard someone screaming behind us. We turned around to find a whole group of people shouting.

"That little girl out there!" I heard someone say, pointing toward the ocean. "She's drowning!"

There were lifeguards on this beach, but I didn't see any of them running to help. In fact, the lifeguard chair nearest to us was empty. But it wouldn't have mattered if there were six lifeguards swimming toward the drowning girl. Frank and I were already racing toward the water.

I could see her now—a little girl of about eight, drifting way out over her head, flailing her arms and screaming for help.

Just as Frank and I were about to dive in, we heard a loud voice behind us.

"EVERYBODY OUT OF THE WATER!"

It was the lifeguard. He was standing on the ladder that led up to his chair, holding on with one hand. In the other he was holding a megaphone.

"Out of the water!" he repeated. "Sharks! Sharks!"

Suddenly, like a human wave, all the people in the water—most of whom had been swimming toward the drowning girl—were turning back and heading for shore.

But not me and Frank. Sharks or no sharks, somebody had to save that little girl's life.

7.

All in a Day's Work

Joe and I are both on the Bayport High swim team. He does short sprints and relays. I hold the school record in the 4 x 400 medley. But it doesn't matter how fast you swim—sharks can swim faster.

The best thing to do was not to think about the danger. We just had to focus on saving that little girl. Every few strokes I'd stop and try to get a bead on where she was. But by the time we were within thirty yards or so, all I saw was the fin, sticking up out of the water.

"You dive down and get her!" I heard Joe shout from somewhere to my right. "I'll fend off the shark!"

I wanted to argue with him, to take on the more dangerous job myself, but there was no time. The little girl's lungs would be full of water by now, and she'd sink like a stone if I couldn't grab her first.

I dove underwater, keeping my eye out for a sinking girl or a swimming shark.

There she was, sure enough. There were still bubbles rising from her mouth and nose, which meant she still had enough air to keep her suspended in the water. But that wouldn't last long.

I strained every muscle in my body to get to her before it was too late.

There!

Throwing her over my shoulder, I held her tight and made for the surface. My own lungs felt like they were going to burst, but I just kept kicking, hoping I'd get some air before I passed out and sent both of us to a watery grave.

I broke the surface just as I was starting to see stars. The world went white for a split second, and then I could hear myself gasping.

Not a peep from the girl, though.

I looked around for Joe, and saw him swimming toward me, holding something by a rope.

A surfboard!

"Some shark," he said as he got near us. "It was turned over, with the fin sticking up."

He brought the board over, and I hoisted the

little girl onto it. Then Joe and I got on opposite sides of the board and swam for shore.

I only hoped it wasn't too late to save our little surfboarder.

No sooner had we got to the beach than a crowd gathered around us. I flipped the girl over onto her stomach and pushed down on her abdominal area. Water gushed out of her mouth. I pushed again, and she started coughing her lungs out.

She was going to make it!

"Make way!" I heard the lifeguard's angry voice barking through the megaphone as he pushed his way through the crowd.

Then he grabbed me by the shoulder. "Back off!" he ordered. "I'll take care of this."

I'm not a hothead by any stretch of the imagination, but nobody—*nobody*—manhandles me and gets away with it. Especially not a lifeguard this dumb. If that girl hadn't still been lying there, needing help, I would have laid into that guy right then and there.

Or maybe not. This guy was a specimen, even for a Jersey Shore lifeguard. From the looks of him, he might well have been a contestant in body-building contests.

He was wearing a thick gold chain around his neck and another around his left wrist—but you could tell that with one flex of his muscles he could have snapped those chains easily.

"Leave my brother alone," Joe said. Next thing I knew, he had pulled the guy away from me and spun him around.

"Hey!" the lifeguard said. "Get your hands off me, punk!" He reared back and let go a left hook that caught Joe smack in the eye—the one that wasn't already blackened.

Now, Joe is a black belt in aikido, and a pretty fair hand at tae kwon do, too—but I know he wasn't thinking straight right then. See, the whole point of the martial arts is to fight with your mind. Not your emotions.

And Joe gets really emotional sometimes. Especially when he's been sucker-punched in the eye. He can get really *angry*.

And who could blame him for being caught off guard? I mean, here we'd just saved this little girl's life. We thought high fives and pats on the back were in order—not the hard time this rockhead lifeguard was giving us.

I could see that Joe was furious. He shook off the pain and squared his body toward his attacker. "Come on," he said. "Let's see you try that again, now that I'm ready for you."

The lifeguard was happy to oblige.

But this time Joe was too quick for him. He ducked out of the way, and at the same time grabbed the guy's arm and helped it along in the direction it was already going.

Then Joe gave a slight yank. The poor slob flipped in midair and came down hard on the sand. The fallen lifeguard muttered something filthy and cracked his knuckles, getting ready for another attack.

"Leave him alone!" one of our blond friends yelled. She stepped right between them. "Those two guys are heroes, you jerk. You should be thanking them!"

"Yeah!" our other friend said. Several others in the tight circle surrounding us agreed.

"Lay off!"

"Put a sock in it!"

"Hey!" the lifeguard yelled, brushing the sand off himself. "Everybody back off! I'm in charge here, and what I say goes!"

"Actually, what *I* say goes."

Everyone turned to see where the booming voice had come from. There stood Bump Rankowski—*Mayor* Bump Rankowski.

"Oh, hi, Mr. Mayor," the lifeguard said, suddenly looking a whole lot smaller and weaker.

"What's going on here?" Bump demanded.

"Um, these two guys disobeyed my orders to clear the water."

"And why'd you order the water cleared?"

"Shark spotting, sir," the lifeguard explained.

"There was no shark, Bump," Joe interrupted. "It was just this surfboard's fin, sticking out of the water. And this little girl was drowning."

The little girl was sitting up by now, with her head tucked between her knees. She coughed every few seconds, but it was easy to see she was going to be all right.

Her mother had found us all by then and was kneeling down, brushing the damp hair out of her daughter's face.

"My baby," she kept saying. "My baby . . . I just went back to our room for a minute. But I could have lost you!"

Well, yeah. Who leaves their little girl on the beach alone for as long as she did?

"What's your name, son?" Bump asked the lifeguard.

"Um, Chuck. Chuck Fatone, sir."

"Chuck Fatone, hmm? I'm gonna remember your name, son," Bump said, shaking a finger at him. "I'd better not hear it again, unless it's to say you saved somebody's life. Understand?"

Fatone gave Joe and me a murderous look

SUSPECT PROFILE

Name: Charles "Chuck" Fatone, aka "Chuckie"

Hometown: Trenton, New Jersey

Physical description: Age 22, 6'3'', 220 lbs. of solid muscle, movie-star suntan, blond, buzz-cut hair, perpetual angry expression on his face.

Occupation: Lifeguard

Background: Grew up tough, got tougher. Likes bodybuilding, being a lifeguard, impressing girls in bikinis. Doesn't like anybody getting in his way. Never married. Never will be. Children? No way.

Suspicious behavior: Not acting faster to save drowning child. Picking a fight with Joe. Just being a generally nasty guy.

Suspected of: Jewel theft, maybe? Bad things (like burglaries) are generally done by bad guys (like Chuckie).

Possible motives: Greed. Rats love cheese, and there's no cheese like expensive bling-bling if you're a rat like Chuckie.

before turning back to the mayor. "Yessir," he said, his mouth twisted into a bitter sneer.

"I hope so," Bump said. Then he turned to the assembled crowd. "All right, everybody. Excitement's over. There was no shark attack. You can rest assured, everything's under control."

Bump's cheerful tone seemed to calm the crowd, and they started to disperse. I could see why he was a successful politician. Everyone just naturally seemed to follow his orders.

"All is well, everyone. Continue having fun on our beautiful beaches. Don't go home without visiting our many fine shops—and make sure you spend lots and lots of money!" At this, he laughed with the crowd. "Oh, and don't forget to use sunscreen!"

With these words the tension was broken. Calm was restored. It was just another wonderful, sunny, hot day at the beach.

"Come on with me, you two," Bump said, throwing an arm around each of our shoulders. "I've got something I want to tell you."

He guided us to a shady spot underneath the boardwalk. Then I felt his grip on my shoulder tighten.

"Listen here," he said. His voice suddenly had a steely note in it. "Trouble seems to follow you boys—first the airplane thing, now this."

"But—"

"Trouble is *not* good for business," he continued. "Not good at all. People don't vacation in places if they're scared a shark will bite them. Got that?"

"But we weren't the ones who—," Joe tried to tell him.

Bump wasn't listening, though. "When the tourists don't come, business gets bad. Really bad."

"But we didn't—"

"And when business gets bad, mayors don't get reelected. *Comprende*?"

What could we say?

"Yes, sir."

"Yes, sir."

"Yes, *Bump*," he reminded us, his best politician's smile flashing back to life. "Call me Bump."

He took out a handkerchief, mopped his brow, and turned back to join the crowd on the beach, waving and smiling at everyone.

"Enjoy, everyone! Enjoy Ocean Point—Pearl of the Jersey Shore!"

8.

Scene of the Crime

Well, *that* was interesting. It was a whole other side of Mayor Bump that we hadn't seen before. There was something else to the guy, underneath his salesman personality. Something gritty and distrusting. It made me wonder what else he knew about the robberies going on in his town—and what he might have reason to hide.

I remembered his words: *"When business gets bad, mayors don't get reelected."*

"Hey, Frank, " I said, "I'll bet if we tell Bump we're here investigating the robberies, he'd have a lot more information to give us."

"Yeah, but we're not going to do that, Joe," he said. "If ATAC wanted him to know, they would have told him we were coming."

Frank was right. We were here undercover, and we'd have to stay that way as long as possible—even if it meant we didn't get access to key information.

And, as our dad says, "There's always another way to get the dirt."

We walked over to a big map bolted to the railing of the boardwalk. Frank fished in his bag and pulled out his PDA. "Let's see," he said, scrolling down with his pointer. "Okay, here are the stores that were robbed. Let's see which is the nearest."

The Shore Thing was the obvious choice—it was just a block off the boardwalk, a little ways south. The other two places were farther down, so we'd be going the right way.

"How's your eye?" Frank asked me.

"Which one?"

There was no way around it—I was now going to have *two* black eyes.

"Guess I should call you raccoon-man," Frank said, snickering.

"Smile a little more when you say that," I said, and headed for a gift shop I'd spotted up ahead. "I'm gonna buy me some shades. Pronto."

I already had a pair for flying, but I'd wanted a pair to just kick around with on the beach, and now seemed the perfect time to go shopping. Within minutes I found a cool pair. Metal. Shiny. Plastic.

"How do I look?" I asked Frank.

In response, he turned and walked away. Who can blame him for being jealous of my looks?

The Shore Thing was not what I'd expected in a jewelry store by the boardwalk. From the fancy awning to the insanely expensive stuff in the display windows, this place reeked of class.

I should have known. Only a place like this could afford to pay for that advertisement engraved in the sand.

"Hey, Frank," I said, catching up to him before he went inside, "how are we gonna handle this?"

"What do you mean?"

"What are we gonna say?"

He smiled. "Leave it to me. Just follow my lead, and let me do the talking."

Okay. Why not? I followed him inside and waited to see Frank's latest game begin.

A bell tinkled somewhere, and this woman came out from the back of the store. Her heels were high, her dress looked like a million bucks—and so did she.

"Can I help you boys?" she asked, giving us the once-over. I could tell by the look in her eyes that she didn't hold out high hopes for us as customers.

"I was looking for a ring for my girlfriend," Frank said.

One of her eyebrows arched. "Aren't you a little young to be thinking about marriage?"

"Oh, no, it's nothing like that," Frank said quickly. "Just a ring—with her birthstone."

"Okay," the woman said, going over to the display cases and opening one up. "What's her birthday?"

"April 1," Frank blurted.

April Fool's Day! Man, he is a smooth liar! He should have been an actor.

What am I saying? He was acting in that store!

"Ah," the woman said with a smile. "She's going to cost you. Diamonds are the birthstone for April."

"D-diamonds?" Frank repeated, sounding like our parrot, Playback. I knew what he was thinking: "Why didn't I pick a different month?"

Guys know nothing about birthstones.

"How about a nice cubic zirconium?" the lady in the dress suggested.

"You mean a fake?" Frank said.

"Well, yes, but a very good one. She'll never know." She gave Frank a wink.

And stupid Frank, instead of saying "Okay," said: "I wouldn't lie to my girlfriend."

The woman laughed, and I could see that Frank had won her over. "Nice boy," she said, patting him on the cheek. "She's a lucky girl."

Frank went beet red. "So, could we see the diamonds?"

She laughed again and went to get a tray of diamond rings to show Frank. "Your friend's a big spender," she told me.

"My brother," I said.

"Don't you ever take those sunglasses off?" she asked me.

"Never," I said.

Okay, it was lame, but what else could I say? I wasn't going to take off my shades and show her my raccoon eyes!

"Ma'am," Frank said, "I heard this store got broken into pretty recently. Is that true?"

She froze. She turned. She gave Frank a long, hard look, decided he wasn't a criminal about to rob her, then brought the tray of diamonds over to him. "True," she said.

I could see that she was still shaken up by what

75

had happened—or by the fact that Frank was asking about it.

"Were you here when the store was broken into?" Frank asked.

"No, it was overnight."

"Huh," Frank said. "Did the police catch the guys?"

"Are you kidding?" she said. "Do they ever catch anybody? They're way too busy giving parking tickets to my customers."

"So was there a big mess?" Frank asked. "Did they break all the windows and stuff?"

"No, not at all," she answered, pushing the tray of diamond rings toward Frank. "Funny, huh? Now, this one's not too expensive. . . ."

Frank examined the ring she was holding up. From where I was standing, about ten feet away, I couldn't even see the stone. It had to be tiny.

"How much is it?"

"Fifteen."

"Fifteen dollars? I'll take it!"

"Fifteen hundred dollars," the woman corrected him.

"Oh," Frank said. "Never mind."

She smiled out of one side of her mouth as she put the ring back. "Maybe something . . . smaller."

"So, about the break-in," Frank said—but he was pushing too hard now.

The woman looked right at him, then at me, and then back at Frank. "You didn't come in here to buy diamonds," she said, her voice suddenly low and hoarse.

"Uh, no, ma'am," Frank said.

"What do you want from me?" She grabbed the tray of diamonds and started backing away toward the display cases. "Why are you asking me all these questions?"

"We're trying to track down the jewel thieves," Frank blurted out. "We're detectives, ma'am."

I couldn't believe it! We were supposed to be undercover here, and he was blabbing about it to a total stranger!

"Private detectives?" the woman asked.

Wisely, Frank let her believe it. She knew too much about us already, if you asked me.

"Yes. We look young for our age. Believe me, we're on your side," Frank told the lady.

She seemed willing to listen—maybe because Frank had made such a nice first impression on her.

"I've already told the police everything," she said. "Why can't you ask them?"

"Ma'am," Frank said, "whatever you told them,

it obviously wasn't enough for them to catch the crooks. There've been two more robberies since, and still no arrests."

"If you know all that, what do you want from me?"

"Why don't you just tell us what happened—from scratch. There might be a little detail in there that the police missed. It could be the key piece of the puzzle—you never know."

She curled over the counter and put her head in her hands. "It had to be an inside job," she said in a low voice. "The security alarm never went off. There were no signs of break-in."

"Who do you think could have done it?" I asked her. "You must have some ideas."

She sighed. "I've thought about it ever since that night. I thought it might be this guy who owns Long John's Silver over on Atlantic Avenue, but then I found out he'd been robbed too—the day before I was."

"Is there anybody else who might know how to beat your security system?" I asked.

"Not that I can think of . . ." Her eyes suddenly clouded over. "Wait a minute." She paused. "No, that's a terrible thought. . . ."

"What?" Frank prodded her.

"I did fire one of my younger employees a few weeks ago, a man in charge of maintenance and cleaning . . . because he kept coming in late. But—"

"It's something," Frank said. "Maybe he was angry and decided to get back at you by robbing the place."

"But why would he rob the other two stores, then?" she asked.

"She's got you there, Frank," I said.

"Well, what's his name, anyway?" Frank said. "We can at least go talk to him."

"I'll give it to you," she said, "but please—don't harass him in any way. He's probably innocent, and I wouldn't want him to be angry at me. . . ."

Something about the way she said this made me think the woman was deathly afraid of her former employee.

"His name is Ricardo Myers."

"Where can we find him?" I asked.

"Well, somebody told me he got a job tattooing up the beach . . . on the pier, I think. You could ask around there."

"Thanks," said Frank, getting up. "We will." He shook her hand. "You've been very helpful . . ."

"Mary," the woman told him. "Mary Fleming.

Here's my card. Please call me if you find anything out."

"You got it," Frank said, and then we were out of there, the little bell tinkling behind us.

I could feel Mary's eyes following us as we headed back toward the boardwalk and the pier.

"What do you think?" I asked Frank.

"About what?"

"About her. Mary Fleming."

"Smart lady."

"Good-looking, too."

"Huh? What's with you today, Joe?"

"Nothing. I just wonder if you let her good looks blind you, that's all."

"Blind me to *what*?"

"Maybe she gave us a good lead," I said. "And *maybe* this guy Ricardo is our man. But it's also possible she's sending us on a wild goose chase. That's all I'm saying."

"Joe, she got robbed," Frank said. "She's a victim, not a suspect."

"She knows we're here investigating," I reminded him.

"So?"

"So, she's now officially dangerous."

"You are *so* weird," Frank said, laughing and shaking his head.

"Hey, Frank. You know what? It's even possible she robbed her own jewelry store."

SUSPECT PROFILE

__Name:__ Mary Fleming

__Hometown:__ New York, NY

__Physical description:__ Age 37, 5'7", 125 lbs., frosted blonde hair, elegant looks, expensive clothes and shoes.

__Occupation:__ Businesswoman

__Background:__ Grew up on Park Avenue, moved to the shore after her divorce. No children. Owns her own business and a house on the beach in nearby Avalon, as well as an apartment in the city where she stays in the winter. Devoted to her business and to making it grow. Drives a hard bargain.

__Suspicious behavior:__ Knows her own security system. A calculating mind and very expensive taste.

__Suspected of:__ Robbing two jewelry stores, plus her own (just to give herself an alibi).

__Possible motives:__ Need or greed—insurance payments can come in very handy.

"What? Why would she do that?"

"I don't know—but there could be a reason. All I know is, there's something about Mary Fleming that I don't like."

9.

X Marks the Spot

Joe is totally nuts, okay?

I don't know, I must have been looking good that week, but for some reason I'd been getting a lot of attention from girls—and women.

And Joe, who now had two—not one, but two—black eyes, was getting more and more jealous by the minute.

I mean, take that poor woman, Mary Fleming. He kept insisting she was some kind of dangerous criminal.

In the past he'd often been right about these hunches of his. But I think this time his black eyes had him seeing things that weren't there.

We got over to the pier in about five minutes.

Most of it was enclosed, and from outside I didn't see any tattoo parlor signs.

"Let's have a look inside," I said.

We did, and we were immediately hit by a wave of noise—dings and rings and blowing horns, and hundreds of human voices, shouting, screaming, laughing. There was the smells of popcorn, salt-water taffy, cotton candy, sunscreen, and people—the good, the bad, and the ugly.

"Hey, Frank, check it out!" Joe said, nudging me and pointing to a sign that read: SOLLY'S SIDESHOW FREAKS. "I've gotta see the sword-swallower—and the bearded lady, too!"

"Later, Joe," I said. "First we talk to Ricardo, okay?"

But Joe was already buying our tickets. He's just too fast for me.

So we went inside, and there were all the freaks and geeks: a guy maybe five feet tall who must have weighed about 800 pounds; a lady with a long beard that looked real and hung down to her belly button; a guy eating fire and swallowing swords; a lady with (if you believed her—and I did) over 500 piercings.

Then I noticed the tattooed man. "I bet he can tell us where to find Ricardo Myers."

I wandered over to the guy. He was busy making muscleman poses so people could snap his picture. His face was covered with tattooed spider webs, and he was in shorts, so everyone could see that his whole body was totally covered with tattoos.

"Wanna take a picture?" he asked me when I reached the front of the little crowd that surrounded him.

"No, thanks," I said. "But can I ask you something?"

"Sure, pal. Go ahead, shoot."

"Doesn't it . . . hurt to get those?"

He laughed. "No pain, no gain."

"Well, what if you wanted to get them removed?"

"Why would I wanna do that?"

I didn't want to upset him, so I just shrugged. "No reason, I guess."

Especially if you *like* being a sideshow attraction.

"Actually, I was thinking of getting a tattoo," I lied. "But I want it done by somebody really good."

"Excellent idea," he said. "Nothing worse than bad art you have to wear."

"I heard about this guy, Ricardo Myers? He's supposed to be good. You know him?"

Tattoo Man smiled and pointed to his face. "He did my spidey-web."

"Cool!" I said. "Know where I can find him?"

"Sure—all the way out on the pier. Place called Rat-a-Tattoo."

Oh yeah—we'd seen that place.

"Thanks!" I said. "Um, keep up the good work!"

I flashed him a thumbs-up and got out of there before I said anything else that would get me into trouble.

"Come on, Joe," I said, dragging him away from the bearded lady. "Let's go find Ricardo."

Rat-a-Tattoo had a psychedelic-style sign above its entrance and a crowd of tattooed and pierced kids hanging out in front.

"Excuse us," I said as we made our way past them. "Coming through."

They stared at us like we were from the moon. A few of them smiled and laughed, thinking we were here to get our first tattoo or piercing.

Inside, we looked around. There were sample drawings hanging from all the walls. You could pick any of these for your tattoo, or bring your own drawing. In the center of the store were cases of rings and pins to stick through whatever hole you had the guys behind the counter poke in you.

There was a curtained doorway, behind which the actual "procedures" were being done, judging by the howls of pain that were coming from back there.

Now, to find Ricardo Myers.

 JOE

Joe here. Frank can be a pretty cool guy, but sometimes he turns into something else.

How should I put it? A geek? A nerd? A totally hopeless loser?

Here we were, in this tattoo palace, surrounded by girls in halter tops that showed off their belly button rings.

And Frank? He was standing there like a frozen yogurt on a stick. This girl was standing right in front of him. She had a tattoo of a shark on her stomach, and she was rolling her belly at him so the shark seemed to swim.

Man, I wished I could take off those shades of mine and introduce myself. Why, that week of all weeks, did I have to get stuck with two black eyes?

I couldn't take any more of this.

I went over to a guy who was, according to the plastic tag on his shirt, the store manager. "That guy over there?" I whispered in his ear. "That's my brother. He wants a nose ring, but he's too shy to ask about it."

"Cool," said the guy, and went over to talk to Frank. I couldn't hear what he said, but Frank looked at him like he was from Mars. Meanwhile, the girl with the shark tattoo moved on, giving up on Frank.

Victory!

"Hey, Frank, come on!" I said, playing like I was him and he was me. "We've got work to do!"

Frank came over. "This place is giving me the creeps," he said. "Let's find Ricardo."

"He's gotta be back there," I said, indicating the curtain.

Over it was a sign reading: EMPLOYEES ONLY. We waited for the manager to turn his back, then sneaked behind it.

Back here, there were little cubicles on either side of a long, brightly lit room. In each cubicle someone was getting pierced or tattooed.

Five of the workers were female. That left three possibilities, and two of them looked like they were at least fifty years old. Mary had said Ricardo was young.

We tried the other guy, who was dressed in shorts and sandals but no shirt. He had a ponytail that hid the tattoo in the middle of his back, but I could see that it was some kind of snake wound around its prey.

This guy was obviously not someone to be messed with.

"Ricardo Myers?" Frank said.

Snake Man looked right at him.

"Who wants to know?"

He left off what he was doing and said to his customer, "I'll be right back." Coming over to us, he said, "Who are you?"

"I'm Frank Hardy, and this is my brother, Joe."

"Yeah? So who sent you?"

"Actually," Frank said, "we're looking into the break-in at The Shore Thing. We wanted to ask you a few questions."

"What are you, cops?"

I could see that Ricardo was getting angry, but the steam wasn't quite coming out of his ears yet.

"Not cops, really," Frank said. "We're sort of checking it out on our own. Turns out some people are saying you might be involved."

"Oh, yeah? Like who?"

"Um, I'm not at liberty to say," Frank told him.

"That Fleming lady," Ricardo said bitterly. "I hate that woman—she's a snob, man. She thinks if you're tough, you must be a criminal."

SUSPECT PROFILE

Name: Ricardo Myers

Hometown: Newark, New Jersey

Physical description: Age 23, 5'7", 160 lbs., hair in ponytail, several tattoos.

Occupation: Tattoo artist, may have mystery occupation on the side.

Background: Grew up in the 'hood, spends summers at the shore. Considered a tattoo artist. Hurting for money, throws away whatever he has by betting it at Atlantic City. Hates rich people and snobs.

Suspicious behavior: His hatred of Mary Fleming and his dread of cops.

Suspected of: Jewel theft.

Possible motives: Revenge on his ex-boss. Need to pay his debts (gamblers often owe lots of money to loan sharks).

"So . . . I guess it's good she fired you, then?" I said.

"Hey! Nobody fires me!" he snapped, grabbing me by the arm. He was so angry, and so strong, that I thought he was going to snap it right off. "Get it?"

"I get it, I get it!" I said. I would have said anything right then, just to make him stop.

Then, just as suddenly as he'd grabbed me, he relaxed his grip and let out a little laugh. "Yeah, man. I like it better here. I make my own hours. Plus I can express myself, y'know? Get into my art."

"How's the pay?" Frank asked.

Good question.

"Stinks." Ricardo's smile vanished.

"How do you get by, then?" Frank asked.

Ricardo's face got ugly in a hurry. "Bug off, okay? It's none of your business how I get by. Mind your own business!"

He gave Frank a shove that sent him into the wall, hard.

Man, talk about mood swings! This guy needed medication, or some serious help.

Frank stayed cool. He just worked out the kinks in his neck and said, "What I really want to ask you, Ricardo, is—"

Just then, the manager lifted the curtain and saw us. "Hey! No customers back here!" he said.

"Oh, sorry," Frank told him. "We're just going."

"Now!"

"Okay, okay," I said, getting between them to give Frank a little more time.

"Here's the question, Ricardo," I heard him say behind me. "Who do you think did it?"

"That's easy. If you're askin' me, I say Mary did it herself."

"Mary?"

"Yeah, man. I bet she ripped off those other two places, then knocked over her own store, just to make herself look innocent."

"Out! Now!" the manager yelled.

"We're going, we're going!" I told him as he shoved us along. "Take it easy, dude. No harm, no foul, okay?"

I heard Ricardo shouting after us. "Hey! If I'd ripped off two million bucks' worth of bling, you think I'd be sitting here doing ankle tattoos for twenty a pop?"

Good point.

With a brief good-bye, we walked out of the shop and headed back down the pier.

"So, what do you think?" I asked Frank.

"Ricardo agrees with you about Mary Fleming. So maybe you're right, Joe. I'll tell you one thing, though—it's hard to think when you're hungry. Let's get some lunch."

"I'm down with that. It's one o'clock already."

We emerged onto the boardwalk and headed for the nearest hot dog stand. We put in our orders and were waiting for our Jersey-style Texas Wieners when we heard screams. Loud screams, coming from the beach.

10.

Buried Treasure

At first we thought it might be somebody drowning, or maybe even a shark attack—a real one this time. But the people who were screaming weren't even near the water. They were in the dry sand, gathered around in a big circle about five deep.

It took us a while to push our way through, and the noise was deafening. Maybe there was a rock star in there, I thought. Poor guy—it sounded like they were tearing him to pieces.

Then we got to the middle of the circle and saw what was really going on.

There was this guy with a metal detector—a truly ugly guy, with hairy moles on his face, really bad teeth, and a scraggly beard.

But that's not what had everybody so crazed.

They were screaming about what he was holding up in his hand: *a huge diamond ring!*

People wanted to get close and see it—the find of a lifetime. They wanted to touch it; to fantasize that they were the ones who'd found it. Metal Detector Man let them get close, but he wouldn't let anyone lay a hand on it.

The crowd was growing, pushing in on us. The rumor must have been racing its way down the beach. Joe was shoved into me, and I banged into the guy on my left. And what do you know, it was Chuck Fatone, the lifeguard! Good thing he wasn't paying attention to us.

"Where'd you find it?" someone asked the lucky man.

"You think I tell you where I find it?" he said in what seemed like an even thicker Russian accent than the taffy man's, and he started laughing his head off.

"I wonder why he told anyone in the first place," I said to Joe. "You'd think he'd have kept it to himself."

"Maybe someone saw him pick it up," Joe said.

"Yeah, I'll bet that's what happened."

"Hey, Frank, I ran into that guy this morning," Joe said. "I meant to tell you about him. He was messing up a really nice sand advertisement."

"A what?"

"An ad drawn in the sand."

"What are you, kidding?"

"Nope—somebody paid to have this ad done in the sand, and that dude messed it up on purpose."

"Hmmm . . ." I said. "That gives me an idea."

I went up to the guy and said, "Excuse me, sir, but I'm from the National Ad Agency, and—"

"What you want?" the guy said in his thick accent.

"This morning you defaced an advertisement of ours. You're going to have to pay for the damage."

"I not pay nothing!"

But before he knew what was happening, I'd snatched the ring from his hand and tossed it to Joe.

"Get a quick look at it!" I yelled as the guy flew at me. "Memorize it, Joe!"

"You not from advertising agency!" the angry Russian yelled, taking a swing at me. I got out of the way just in time. "You crook! Give me back diamond ring!"

"Here you go, buddy," Joe said, tossing the ring back to him. "Nice diamond—congratulations."

The guy snatched the ring out of the air and went to pick up his metal detector. Then he turned back to me. "If I see you again . . ." he said, and pretended to slit his throat with his finger.

I got the message loud and clear. And hopefully, if Joe had gotten a good look at the ring, I wouldn't need to bother him again.

"Well?" I asked him as we backed away from the crowd.

"About two karats, I'd guess. Brand new. And it had an inscription on the inside in cursive: 'Melissa & Fred 4 ever.' With the number 4."

"Good job, Joe."

"So you think it's one of the stolen items?"

"I don't know, but it shouldn't be too hard to find out. Come on."

"Where we going?"

"Back to The Shore Thing."

"Why not check the other two places first?"

"That was an expensive ring," I said. "And The Shore Thing seems to specialize in pricey stuff."

JOE

Joe here. Mary Fleming didn't seem happy to see us. Not until we told her about the ring on the beach. After that, she was all action. She checked in her inventory book, and then in her ledger of current orders.

"Yes, here it is—it was scheduled to be picked up today. 'Melissa & Fred 4 ever.'"

"Whoever stole it must have dropped it," Joe said.

A reasonable guess, I had to agree. At that moment it occurred to me that the ring was found on the beach, right near the pier where Ricardo Myers worked.

Hmmm . . .

"Thanks, Ms. Fleming," I said. "We'll try to get the ring back for you."

"Thank *you,* boys!" she said, waving good-bye. "Thank you very much!"

She seemed happy about it, which I took as a good sign. If she'd stolen her own stuff, it wasn't likely she'd have dropped it on the beach, and it was even less likely that she'd be happy it was found.

Ricardo Myers had tried as hard as he could to point the finger at her. I wondered what more was going on there. What did he really have against her—and how far had he gone to get even?

We went back to the spot on the beach where the crowd had been. There was no sign of our ugly Russian friend with the metal detector.

The crowd had broken up, but all along that part of the beach, people were on their knees, screaming and yelling.

And digging.

Not far from us, a large, dark-haired girl was gouging away with a beach shovel she must have stolen from some poor little kid.

"Hey!" I called to her. "What's going on?"

She looked up at me, her eyes wide and wild.

"You'd better start digging!" she said.

"Digging for what?"

She grinned from ear to ear. "So far they've found three diamond rings and a silver bracelet in the sand!"

11.
Gold Rush

If you've never seen a whole crowd of people go crazy, let me tell you—it is an incredible sight.

People on the beach were running in every direction. As soon as they found what they thought was a "lucky spot," they dropped to their knees and started digging.

Word must have been spreading, too, because more and more people kept coming down from the boardwalk to the beach. Some of them already had shovels or magnifying glasses. Everyone was screaming and shouting.

Can we say "madhouse"?

It was the California gold rush all over again!

"Hey, Joe," Frank said, nudging me with his elbow. "Check it out."

He nodded toward a big knot of people. I had to crane my neck to see what was going on.

Looked like everyone was crowding around some guy who was selling *metal detectors*! This guy had a little stand set up, and he was selling detectors as fast as he could take people's money.

"That guy is some kind of businessman," I said.

"Joe," Frank said, "doesn't it strike you as a little odd?"

"Odd?"

"Somebody finds a ring, and fifteen minutes later, this guy's got enough metal detectors to make a killing selling them? You think that's a coincidence?"

"I guess it is kind of strange."

"Come on," Frank said. "Let's go find out how he got so lucky."

It took a little while to get to the front of the line. Nobody likes people who cut. But our instant tycoon wasn't going anywhere—not while his supply of metal detectors held out.

From the looks of it, he must have brought a whole truckload of them. "How did he get them here so fast?" I wondered out loud.

"Maybe he knew there would be a jewelry hunt."

"Huh?"

"If he stole the stuff himself, he could have

planted it here, knowing somebody was bound to find it. Then all he had to do was be ready with his merchandise."

"Yeah, but Frank, he didn't even *have* to do that. He could have just taken off with the stolen jewelry. Why even bother?"

Frank, as usual, was ready with an answer: "Because it's hard to find a buyer for stolen jewelry. Remember, that first ring was engraved. And the store owners must have put out a list with descriptions of the stolen merchandise. Jewelry is unique. It can be tracked. Even pawnshops would be given the list by the police, and they'd be watching for stolen goods."

My reasoning still led me to think it would be easier and more profitable to just steal the jewels and run.

We were edging closer, and now we could hear our man shouting at a customer.

"I don't give bargain!" he was saying. "You want bargain, go someplace else! Here, is one price fits all. You buy, or no buy, what I care?"

Hmmm . . . our man had a thick Russian accent, just like the guy who found the first ring. There seemed to be quite a community of Russians here in Ocean Point—the saltwater taffy man, these other two . . .

I wondered if maybe they were all in this together.

"Frank, it could be the Russian Mafia!"

I felt like I'd stumbled onto the solution. With one stroke of pure genius, I'd cracked the case!

"Easy, there, Joe. Just because three people have the same accent, it doesn't make them all criminals."

My bubble instantly burst, and I came back down to Earth. "I guess you're right. But you've got to admit, it's a possibility."

"One of *several*. We'll add it to our list, okay?"

"You want buy?" the Russian guy asked us. We'd reached the front of the line.

"What we want," I said, "is to know how you knew to show up here just in time to cash in on this treasure frenzy."

The guy scowled at me. He had a big, bushy mustache that drooped down on either side of his mouth, and his gray hair was long and wild. He obviously hadn't combed it in a *very* long time.

"You shut face, okay?" he said to me. "Why it's your business what I do? Is free country!"

"You've got to admit," Frank said, "it *is* pretty suspicious looking, your getting here so fast."

"What you are, junior police officers?" the man asked, sticking his chin out at Frank, then at me. "I

103

come to this country to make decent living and be free. Not to live in police state, okay? Now, get lost. In this country, I have right to sell what I want."

"Nobody's arguing with that, sir," Frank said, trying to calm the guy down.

"Is free enterprise!"

"Yes, sure . . . um, what's your name, sir?"

"None of your business."

"No, of course not. I just wanted to call you by your name, that's all. My name's Frank Hardy, and this is my brother, Joe."

The guy made a face, but decided to back down a little. "Vladimir Krupkin," he said, and gave us a little nod. "Now get lost, okay? I busy now. You want talk, come back later."

"Just one question, Vladimir," Frank said, "and then we'll leave you alone, okay?"

Vladimir looked at the crowd behind us. "Make quick," he said.

"You were right about us," Frank admitted. "We *are* kind of junior police officers. And the thing is, we know that some of the jewelry people are finding was stolen from local jewelry stores."

Vladimir crossed his arms on his chest. "Really?" He didn't look one bit surprised. "So you think I steal jewelry, then bury in sand, then come here to sell metal detectors?"

SUSPECT PROFILE

<u>Name:</u> Vladimir Krupkin

<u>Hometown:</u> Moscow, Russia

<u>Physical description:</u> Age 45, 5'10", 220 lbs., graying, uncombed hair, pot belly.

<u>Occupation:</u> Opportunist. Something different every time you look.

<u>Background:</u> Grew up in Russia, came to America to escape Communism. When Communism fell, he didn't go back because he'd gotten several good rackets going.

<u>Suspicious behavior:</u> Showing up on the beach with a ready-made business to exploit an opportunity he couldn't have known was coming unless he was in on the thefts.

<u>Suspected of:</u> Conspiracy involving jewel theft.

<u>Possible motives:</u> Money.

Then he let out a laugh so loud you could hear it in Atlantic City. "You think Vladimir is such a stupid? Why I steal jewelry and then throw away? Is crazy! Ha!"

He had a point—it didn't make any sense. But

then, nothing about this case was making much sense. Yet.

We could still hear him laughing as we climbed the stairs to the boardwalk.

"I can't think when I'm hungry," I said to Frank.

"That's right—we never got our Texas wieners!"

We ate our lunch, topped off by some of the best soft ice cream cones we'd ever had, and tried to get our heads straight about this case.

"Mmmm," I said, licking off the chocolate drips before they fell on my shorts. "Nothing like ice cream for clearing the mind."

"Mmmm," said Frank, nodding in agreement.

"So—something's rotten in Ocean Point."

"Definitely."

"But what? And who's behind it?"

"That *is* the question."

"So what's the answer? Got any ideas?" I asked.

Stupid question. Frank *always* has ideas.

"Let me ask you this, Joe: Who would benefit if a bunch of people found jewelry lying around the beach?"

"Um, the people who found the stuff?"

Frank rolled his eyes. "Besides them."

"Okay, um . . ." I stared at my dripping ice cream cone. Then it hit me. "Ice cream vendors!"

"Right. And?"

"Hot dog stand owners, and tattoo parlors, and hotel owners, and parking lot owners, and restaurants, and clubs . . ."

"Exactly. And so on. If thousands of people want to come to a place, prices go up, and all the local businesses profit."

"And your point is . . . ?"

Frank smiled. "It's the one motive that explains everything that's happened so far."

"Yeah, sure. The only problem is there are hundreds of merchants in Ocean Point, and they'd probably all benefit—"

"—except the jewelry stores, maybe. But they'd get their insurance money," Frank finished.

"Right. How are we going to figure out which one of them is behind the scheme?"

Frank nodded. "Or which *ones*? It could be a bunch of them working together in a conspiracy."

"So how do we narrow it down?"

All this time we'd been working on our cones, and Frank had now finished his. He bought a bottled water and used some of it to wash his sticky hands. Then he handed it to me, because I was more of a mess than he was.

"I don't think," he said, "that a little popcorn stand or souvenir store owner would throw away millions of dollars of jewelry just to increase tourism. Only a very wealthy person could afford to throw away gold and diamonds. Anyone else would try to turn it into straight cash."

"Okay. That still leaves us with a lot of people as suspects—and most of them we haven't even met yet."

Frank didn't answer. Instead, he turned around and started talking to the ice cream vendor, an older guy who looked like he'd been around here forever.

"Excuse me, sir."

"Yeah?"

"Do you own this place?"

"Me?" The guy laughed—a big, hearty belly laugh. "I don't own the shirt on my back, kid."

"Well, who does own it?"

"Same guy who owns half the shops and restaurants on the boardwalk—Carl Jardine."

"Carl Jardine? Is he the richest man in town?"

"Oh, by far," the guy told Frank. "He's a multigazillionaire. You'd think he'd spread it around a little—give his workers health benefits or something—but no. He just uses his money to buy up more stuff."

The guy was on a roll now. Frank just let him go on, nodding once in a while to show he understood and sympathized.

It's amazing how being a good listener makes people open up to you and talk their heads off.

"You think he works hard, like everybody else? No way!" the man said, his voice starting to get a little loud. "No, he spends all his time on the beach, building sand castles and stuff."

Frank chuckled.

"You think I'm kidding?" the man added. "That's him right down there! You don't believe me, go see for yourself!"

12.

The Richest Man in Ocean Point

We walked over to the railing near the beach and scanned the area, expecting to see a man building a sand castle.

What we saw was the Taj Mahal.

I kid you not—this sculpture was so big that the man building it looked like a midget next to it. He could barely reach the top of the Taj's tower to finish it off. In fact, he was standing on a big cooler to do it.

We thanked the ice cream man for his time and headed over to meet the richest man in town.

The closer we got to it, the more incredible Jardine's sand sculpture was. The thing was the size of a small house, but it was the details that were really amazing.

I'd seen pictures of the Taj Mahal—a tomb built by an emperor for his lady love. A lot of people say it's the most beautiful building ever built.

Jardine had done it proud, down to the lakes and gardens that surround the building. The lakes even had water in them! He must have lined them with something so the water wouldn't drain out.

Fascinating. I wondered about the mind of this man. It was obviously brilliant and talented, but was it also the mind of a criminal?

"Mr. Jardine?" I said.

"Yes?"

"I'm Frank Hardy, and this is my brother, Joe. We're Junior Chamber of Commerce members in our home town, Bayport, and we're doing a piece for the September edition of our high school paper. . . ."

"Oh, you want to interview me, huh?" he said, squinting up at us.

He had to be seventy years old, but Carl Jardine was still in good shape. He wore a beach hat, bathing suit, and flip-flops, and his skin was tanned and leathery. This guy had spent a lot of time in the sun. But he had a pretty good build for an older guy.

"All right, why not?" he said. "That's pretty good, tracking me down on the beach like this. I like initiative. Key to success!"

SUSPECT PROFILE

Name: Carl Jardine

Hometown: Asbury Park, New Jersey

Physical description: Age 72, 6'2", 200 lbs., gray hair, leathery skin, well-preserved older man.

Occupation: Retired. Or is he . . . ?

Background: Grew up in Asbury Park, moved to Ocean Point as a young man. Bought first taffy stand at twenty-three. Now owns dozens of properties and businesses. No one knows what he does with all his money, except to buy more businesses. Could his empire have a shaky foundation? One that needs shoring up with illegal schemes?

Suspicious behavior: Mostly circumstantial. He fits the profile, spends lots of time on the beach, and wouldn't blink at throwing away tens of thousands of dollars worth of jewelry just to bring in more customers to his many, many businesses.

Suspected of: Seeding the sand with stolen jewelry. Lying about it.

Possible motives: Money, money, and more money. Some folks can never have enough.

He kept working as he spoke. I don't know what he thought he was doing; his Taj Mahal looked pretty perfect as it was.

"This is incredible!" Joe said, meaning the sculpture.

"Did it all myself," Jardine said. "I do everything myself. Only way to get something done right!"

"I understand you're the richest man in Ocean Point?" I said, trying to steer the conversation around to our case.

"I wouldn't know about that. I don't go counting other people's money."

"You don't need to count it if you're throwing it away—or burying it in the sand." Joe muttered the last part under his breath. But it wasn't quiet enough for my taste.

But if Jardine had heard him, he didn't let on. "I've done pretty well, though. Got quite a few businesses going, but they mostly run themselves at this point. I collect the checks and put them in the bank. I'm seventy-two years old—I've got more important things to do than work in an office."

He scraped a bit of extra sand off one of the Taj's walls.

"How did you get started in business?" I asked him.

"My first venture was a little saltwater taffy store on the boardwalk," he said. "I've still got that place. Rented it out to a Russian fella." He fell silent, and started inspecting his work for any stray grains of sand.

"So, you were saying . . . ?" I prompted him.

"Well, saltwater taffy was big in those days. We didn't have fast-food places on our boardwalk back then, or ice cream shops. I was one of the first attractions. I had a couple dozen taffy places all up and down the shore. Now I've got lots of other businesses as well."

"Would you say you have any enemies in town?" I asked.

"Enemies? Well, I guess you don't buy up half a town without running into some opposition. To win those kinds of battles you have to be strong."

He laughed. "Put that in your article! Tell them I'm retired now, doing what I love. I've done over fifty of the world's great buildings in sand, and I've got lots more to go before I sleep. And tell your readers I'm a man at peace with myself. I wish everyone the best, and I just want to be left alone."

I could appreciate that, but we had a job to do. There was no way we could leave him alone—not when he fit our suspect profile better than anyone else we'd come across.

We'd gotten as far as we could with the teen reporter jive. It was time to level.

"I'll be honest with you, sir," I said. "We're actually looking into the jewelry store robberies that happened here recently."

"You're . . . not really interviewing me for an article?" He seemed disappointed.

"Not for our school paper, no," I admitted. "You see, sir, we figure that whoever's been scattering the stolen jewelry on the beach for people to find, they must not have much need for the cash that jewelry could bring."

"Ah," he said. "Someone like me, eh?"

"I'm afraid so."

"You think I robbed those stores and buried thousands of dollars in jewelry to create a tourist boom, out of which people like me would make millions. Is that right?"

"More or less," I said.

"Let me tell you something, young fellows," he said, stopping work for the first time since we'd arrived. "I understand your theory. I can see that you've given it some thought. But you've got the wrong culprit. I have so much money that I have no need to make more. I already have more than I could spend in a lifetime. I'm a happy man. So if you'll please leave me alone, I'd like to get back to work."

Oh, well. At least he thought it was a good theory.

"Sir, one more thing," I said. "You've been around here a long time, and you know a lot of people. Who do *you* think is behind it?"

Jardine knitted his bushy eyebrows. "I think," he said, "that your theory is fundamentally sound. But you need to adjust your sights lower—to a level of wealth lower than my own, but not at the bottom of the ladder, if you know what I mean. Go find a list of the members of the Chamber of Commerce or something. That ought to get you started."

"How many people do you think are on that list?" Joe asked.

"Dozens, I should imagine."

"Frank, how are we ever going to interview them all? We've only got a few days to figure this out before we have to go home."

"You might as well forget it, then," Jardine said, turning back to his work. "You'll never find the ones behind it. To catch them, you'd have to monitor this beach day and night!"

I pulled Frank aside for a moment. "We could do that, right?" I said. "It would save us our hotel bill if we camped out on the beach."

"Forget it," Jardine said. He must have overheard me. "There's no camping allowed in Ocean Point. The boardwalk lights go off at 3 A.M., and it's dark as pitch out here after that, especially when there's a new moon, like tonight. How would you even see anyone in the dark?"

He turned back to his Taj Mahal, and Joe and I looked at one another excitedly.

Carl Jardine was right—it would be dark as pitch. But what he didn't know was that, courtesy of ATAC, we had a night vision telescope!

The richest man in Ocean Point had given us our next plan of action: an all-night stakeout on the beach.

13.
Stakeout!

We went back to our hotel and tried to get a couple hours of sleep before dinner. We were going to be up all night, after all, and we didn't want to fall asleep on the job.

When we woke up, it was around 6 P.M., and we were both hungry. We got dressed, packed all our overnight essentials in a backpack, and headed downstairs to get some dinner.

We were waiting for our food to come and going over the case when I spotted the two blondes from the beach. They were in jeans and tank tops now, but they were still unmistakable.

I just hoped they didn't see us. I'd left my shades in the room, figuring I wouldn't need them overnight on the beach. But I hadn't figured on this. The last thing I wanted was them seeing me with *two* black eyes.

"Yoo-hoo! Frank!"

Ugh. Too late.

They came right over to our table and sat down with us. The girl next to Frank nudged up really close to him—so close that he moved in toward the wall of the booth a little, edging away from her out of sheer embarrassment.

The girl on my side of the table didn't move in on me at all. Instead, she leaned over the table toward Frank.

The one across the table gave me a look. "Eeeuw!" she squealed. "Look at your eyes!"

Her friend next to me took a close look. "Omigosh, you look like a—"

"I know, a raccoon," I said.

"Right!"

"That lifeguard socked you pretty good," the girl across the table said.

"Hey, I didn't know it was coming," I said, defending myself.

It would have been nice of Frank to say something right about then, but he was so shy in the presence of these two girls that he never opened his mouth.

"You should have decked him," the girl next to me said.

"Yeah," the other agreed. "You really wimped out."

I was about to argue with her, but just then our food arrived.

"So, Frank, what are you doing tonight?" the girl next to him asked.

"Um, Joe?" Frank looked at me pleadingly. Obviously, he didn't know what to say.

"We're, uh . . . spending the evening with our parents," I said.

Talk about wimping out. But it worked.

"Your parents? Ick. Sounds totally boring. We're going clubbing."

"Really?" I said. "Have a nice time."

"Oh, we will," said the girl across from me. "I don't know about you, though."

Finally, they got up and left, and we were able to eat our meal in peace. "Do me a favor, Frank," I said, "next time we're on a case, try to stay away from romantic entanglements."

"Romantic entanglements?"

"Whatever, just steer clear, okay?"

I guess I was being a little hard on him. After all, it was me who introduced us to the girls, not him. Still. How frustrating was this?

"Come on," Frank said as we pushed away our dessert plates. "Let's go nail us a criminal."

• • • •

By eight o'clock the beach was deserted, except for one or two couples strolling hand in hand as the sun went down.

Frank and I both agreed that no one would be planting jewelry on the beach in broad daylight. We also agreed that the most likely time would be after 3 A.M., when the boardwalk lights would go off, plunging the beach into almost total darkness.

We had a long time to wait. We probably didn't need to be out here yet, but we didn't want to miss anything if it happened earlier than we thought. We took up positions under the boardwalk, and Frank fished out the night vision scope from the backpack.

"Okay," he said as he snapped it open and scanned the empty beach. "Bring it on."

"Well?" I asked. "What do you see?"

"Just a few drunks . . . some couples making out . . . there's a guy fishing . . . uh, a bunch of seagulls . . . a homeless guy . . ."

"All right, all right, never mind. Just tell me when you see something interesting."

Frank smiled at me. "You'll get your turn, little brother. Just be patient."

I *hate* when he calls me "little brother." He's only eleven months older than me, you know. And I look older and more mature.

Anyway, hours went by. I was sorry I hadn't brought my MP3 player to pass the time. Ten o'clock, eleven, midnight, one . . . and still two hours to go before prime time! This was truly going to rank among the most boring nights of my life—especially if our criminal didn't show up.

At three o'clock all the lights went out. Suddenly, I couldn't see my hand in front of my face. It took all of about ten minutes before I could make out Frank, still staring through the scope at the beach.

"Am I going to get a turn, or are you just going to hog that thing?" I asked.

"Here," he said, giving it to me. "If you're going to keep on nagging me about it . . ."

"We're supposed to share," I reminded him. "They only gave us one of these."

That got him. He sat down and lapsed into silence. The only sound now was that of the waves crashing in.

The spot we'd chosen for our stakeout looked out on the stretch of beach where the first ring had been found. Most of the jewelry had been dug up within view of our position. The town pier was on our left, maybe fifty yards away.

I was looking that way, peering through the scope, when I thought I saw something move.

Maybe it was just a homeless guy, prowling for crabs to eat or a place to sleep.

Or maybe not.

I nudged Frank. "Under the pier," I whispered. "Something moving."

"Let's go check it out," he said.

Still staring through the scope, I emerged from our hiding place and headed toward the pier with Frank on my right, holding on to my arm because he couldn't see where he was going.

Suddenly he let out a grunt, and I felt him let go of my arm.

"What the—?"

Then I felt something hard come down on the back of my head. As I crumpled to the sand, all I could see were stars.

FRANK

14.

Neck-Deep in Trouble

Joe was down—I could see that much.

I was down too, but not out. I struggled to my feet and swung.

Within seconds, my right fist plowed into something soft.

"Ooof!"

A massive shape in front of me doubled over, and I kicked hard at it.

Then I was jumped from behind—by not one, but two guys. The second got his hands around my throat.

I tried to wrestle the second guy off me, but he wouldn't budge.

Meanwhile, the guy I'd brought down before was slowly recovering. He got to me before I could get free of his friend, and socked me so hard in the stomach that I thought I was going to lose my dinner.

I sank to the ground and felt a series of hard kicks delivered to my kidneys. I tried to protect my face and to make the rest of me as small a target as possible. It hurt—but I could sense my attackers getting tired. And it wasn't anything I couldn't handle.

"Tie them up!" the other man said.

Rope was wound around my hands, and the guy was busy tying them behind my back when I heard a loud "Oof!" and he let go.

"Get away from my brother, screwball!"

Joe was back in the fight!

My hands were now tied too tightly for me to help. The two other assailants quickly ganged up on Joe. I heard a loud *crack,* and then Joe yelling, "Ow! My eye!"

He has the worst luck sometimes.

Another minute or two and Joe was lying beside me on the ground, getting his hands tied in the same style as mine.

"Should I bash their heads in?" one of them asked the other.

"Nah," one of his companions answered. "No marks, remember? Now go over behind that piling and get the shovel."

I tried to place their voices, but they weren't familiar. As for their faces, there was no way to make them out in the pitch darkness. Not without our night scope, and who knew where that had fallen?

"Shovel?" the first guy repeated. He didn't sound too bright. "We gonna bury something?"

"Yeah, lamebrain. We're gonna bury these two—alive."

I could see now where things were heading, and it wasn't anyplace good. From the sound of the waves hitting, we were right near the waterline. And it was low tide. If they buried us here—and they were already digging the hole—all traces of digging would be wiped out by the rising tide before the sun came up. No one would ever find us until the day—years from now, maybe—when a hurricane or nor'easter rearranged the beach and made the dead rise.

Once the hole was deep enough, we were both thrown in alive, and they started to shovel the sand back in. When they were done, only our heads were above the sand.

Whoever was doing this wanted us to suffer before we died. Hmmm . . . we must have been annoying somebody pretty badly. To me it meant that our investigation was coming close. Too close for a bad guy's comfort.

And mine, too, actually. The water didn't look too great from this vantage point.

"Who are you?" I asked the men who'd accosted us. "Why are you doing this?"

I didn't think I'd get an answer, but it was worth a try—especially since at least one of them didn't seem too bright.

"None of your business," the answer came back from the darkness.

"Who hired you?"

"What makes you think somebody hired us?" the voice said. "Maybe we're just doing this for fun."

"Fun? You think this is fun?" Joe raged.

"Sure! I can just picture you two as the tide comes up. You'll drown real slow . . . if the dogs and vultures don't get you first! Hahahaha!"

"Hahahaha!" came the echoing laugh of one of his companions. They sounded like hyenas.

"Wait," I said calmly. "Whatever you're being paid, we can double it."

"Oh, I doubt it. I doubt it very much. We're going to make a killing on this one! Hahahaha!"

"Hahahaha!"

"Come on, guys—let's leave these two alone. They've got a lot of thinking to do . . . about how curiosity killed the cat! Hahahaha!"

"Hahahaha!"

The laughter was driving me nuts.

Within seconds they were gone, taking their shovel—our only hope of escape—with them.

For a few moments there was dead silence. Then Joe spoke up. "My nose itches."

There was no sense in telling him to scratch it. This sand was hard packed. We weren't going to just slip out like we would from dry sand.

And did I mention we were tied, hands and feet? Not good.

"How's the rest of you?" I asked.

"I got punched in the eye again."

"Oh, no."

"Same one the cow kicked."

"Ouch."

"Oh, well. At least now I won't have to worry about how it looks."

There was another long silence. Then:

"Does this remind you of anything?" Joe asked.

"Yeah. Farmer Pressman's grain bin."

"Ding-ding-ding! Yes, that's right, for one hundred dollars!"

"Only now we're buried much deeper," I added helpfully.

"And we have no gizmos to help us."

"And our hands aren't free, let alone our legs."

"So, we're history, right?"

"Wrong!" I said. "Don't give up, Joe. I'll think of something."

I think he believed me. Joe has a lot of faith in my mental powers. But right at that moment, I myself didn't have much faith in them. In fact, I didn't have a clue.

15.

Miracles from on High

We were buried up to our necks, about six feet from the waterline, and the waves kept breaking closer and closer to our heads. I was having flashbacks to our grain bin rendezvous. I hadn't really wanted a repeat performance so soon.

"I just want to say, Frank, that it's been awesome having you for a brother."

I don't know what made me say that. Of *course* we were going to get out of this. Frank was going to think of something at the last minute, and it would all be okay.

But Frank didn't look too happy. He was busy spitting out the salt water he'd just swallowed. High tide was fast approaching.

And so was something else.

"Frank, look!"

The way we were buried, I could see the light easier than Frank could. But we could both hear the sound of the engine. It was coming straight for us.

"What is it?" I asked.

He squinted his eyes to protect them from the glare of the light. "Can't see what kind of vehicle it is . . . but it must be one of those machines that rake up the garbage at night."

Frank and I both screamed as loudly as we could, hoping to get the attention of the driver. The light seemed to turn our way and get brighter. The machine kept coming, and the engine was now drowning out both the surf and our screams.

"We're saved!" Frank kept shouting like an idiot. "We're saved!"

I wasn't so sure. It was pitch dark out here, and in spite of the headlights, the driver might not see our heads poking out of the sand. He might just mistake our heads for plastic garbage bags or something, and rake them up into the jaws of his machine.

Our cries for help became screams of terror as the "grim reaper" descended on us. There was no way the driver could possibly hear us over the roar of the vehicle's engine.

Then, at the last second, there was a shriek of

brakes. The metal monster came to a stop about three feet from our heads.

As if that weren't enough, a big wave chose that very moment to crash over us. When it retreated, we were left gasping and coughing.

Help came in the form of a beautiful dark angel's face, bending over mine. "Whoa!" the angel said. "What the . . . What are you two doing here?"

Good question.

"It's a long story," Frank said. "But we haven't got much time. Could you please just dig us out first?"

"Um, yeah, sure," the angel said. "You're lucky I've got a shovel in there."

She went over to her tractor and came back with one. She started digging Frank out while I had to chill, holding my breath whenever the waves came crashing over me.

Pretty soon Frank was able to use his arms to haul himself out. Then the two of them came over to dig me up.

Her name was Naomi, she told us—Naomi Thompson. She was wearing sweats, and her hair was done in cornrows. She was the one who embossed the advertisements in the sand, using her tractor and its nifty rear attachment to make those amazing drawings.

"You're lucky I spotted you," she said. "I just happened to be circling back around, or I wouldn't have had my lights pointed so close to the water."

"Well, thanks for saving us," Frank said.

"No problem. Are you gonna tell me how you wound up like that?"

"Sure," I said. "How about we tell you all about it over lunch tomorrow?"

She gave me a look. "I've heard that line before. How 'bout you tell me first, and *then* we decide about lunch?"

So we told her everything we knew. She's been out on the beach every night; if anybody'd been out there, scattering jewelry in the sand for tourists to find, Naomi might have seen him—or her.

But no. Apparently, it had been pretty quiet. "I've seen a lot of weird stuff poking out of the sand since I started working here," she said. "That's why I bring the shovel with me. But I've never seen anything as weird as two guys' heads."

We borrowed her shovel and filled the two holes back up. That way, in case anyone came by the next day to check on us, they wouldn't know we'd escaped.

"Well now," I said to Naomi when we were done. "What about our lunch date?"

"Um, Joe," Frank said quickly. "Let me remind you about something."

"Huh?"

"Whoever tried to kill us—at this point, they think we're dead."

"Yeah? So?"

"If we want them to keep thinking that, we can't go around in broad daylight, taking girls out to lunch in restaurants."

"Sorry, Naomi," I said, realizing he was right.

"That's okay. Maybe after your eyes heal up."

Ouch. Forgot about those.

She got back into the driver's seat. "Gotta get back to work."

"Where can we find you?" I asked.

"Me? I'm out here every night, from 3 A.M. to 5 A.M. Princess of Darkness, that's me."

She revved up the engine and put the tractor in gear. Soon she was just a spot of light retreating up the beach.

"So," I said. "We're ghosts, huh? Cool."

"Yeah," Frank said with a smile. "You know, for a ghost, I feel pretty alive."

"Me too. Thanks to Naomi."

Frank looked up at the stars. "Yeah, good thing she came by, or we'd probably be sunk." He paused for a moment. "Great night, huh?"

I looked up at the sky. And suddenly, something hit me.

Hard.

Smack in the forehead.

"What the—?"

16.

A Bump on the Head

I heard something smack Joe on the head, and an instant later, his cry of pain.

"Ow!"

I turned around, ready to drop-kick whoever was attacking us.

But there was no one there at all!

Something had knocked Joe in the head. There was no doubt about that. He was on his knees, holding his forehead.

"Are you all right?" I asked him.

"Dang, that hurts!"

"Are you bleeding?"

He checked. "I don't think so—but I'm gonna have a lump the size of a—"

He broke off and reached down for something that was lying in the sand. "Hey, Frank—check this out. This must be what hit me!"

He held it up, and I took it from him. It was a heavy gold bracelet—the kind that locks together and looks like you could attach a heavy chain to it.

But where had it come from?

We were down by the water—too far from the boardwalk or the pier for someone to have thrown it. And there was no one near us on the beach, at least as far as we could see in this darkness just before dawn. Besides, to make such an impact, that bracelet had to have come from a really far distance. . . .

Then we heard it—the drone of an engine high above us. I looked up, and there it was: the red blinking lights of an airplane.

Suddenly, all the pieces of the jigsaw puzzle began to come together in my mind.

So *that* was how the pieces of jewelry were finding their way onto the beach!

"Joe," I said, "who do we know around here that has a plane?"

"Bump," he said, feeling the one on his forehead. "Bump Rankowski."

"Exactly. He's got a whole fleet of planes, he

said. He employs pilots to fly them up and down the beach during the day. But what if he paid those pilots *extra,* in *cash,* to do a little night work—say at 3 or 4 A.M., digging a couple of holes on the beach?"

"Could be," Joe agreed. "And he's got motive, too, Frank—more tourists on the beach means more advertising business, right?"

"Not to mention the real motive—that, as the mayor, he'd benefit from a big rise in tourism. It would make him *very* popular with the local business owners—except, of course, the ones he's been robbing!"

"We've gotta nail this guy," Joe said, gritting his teeth and rubbing the swelling bump on his noggin.

Was this about catching a criminal, or about nailing the guy who kept beating Joe up? I couldn't tell, but I figured I'd hit the ball into his court for a change.

"So how are you planning to nail Bump?" I asked.

"Huh?"

"You're so eager to get him in cuffs, how are you going to do it? You've got to have proof, remember?"

Joe frowned, and rubbed his forehead. "Isn't this proof enough?"

"Nope."

"Yeah. I guess not."

I suddenly found myself yawning. It dawned on me that we'd been up all night. It had been a long day, to say the least.

"Why don't we sleep on it, Joe?"

"Sleep?"

"Yeah, sleep—remember it? I, for one, happen to think better when I'm not dog tired. Besides, Bump—if he's our guy—thinks we're dead, right? If we want him to keep thinking that, we'd better get out of sight before sunrise."

"We're going to have to show our faces eventually," Joe said.

"Yeah," I agreed. "But not until we've got a plan."

 **JOE**

Joe here. So we snuck back to our hotel room without anyone seeing us. It wasn't hard—at 5 A.M. there aren't many people out and about. Bump would probably still be out at the airport.

I got a bag of ice from the machine in the hallway and put it on my face, which was hurting all over.

Frank was out cold and snoring, but I was so tired that I managed to fall asleep anyway.

He had set the alarm for 10 A.M. Five hours isn't much, but I felt a whole lot better when I woke up, I can tell you that.

Frank went down the hall and got us some breakfast from the vending machines. Donuts and tarts, mmm mmm. Now *that's* my kinda breakfast!

We sat out on beds, eating and trying to come up with a plan of action.

"We've got to be sure it's him first," Frank said, munching on a frosted donut.

"You're not sure? *I'm* sure!"

"I'm pretty sure. But I don't want us to take down somebody and then find out that they're innocent. That would compromise ATAC."

"All right. So what should we do next?" I asked.

"Well, I think we should do an Internet search— see if it tells us anything."

"Okay. Only we didn't bring a laptop. What do you want to do? Go to Bump's office and ask him if we can borrow his computer?"

I was being sarcastic, obviously. But Frank gets oblivious sometimes, especially when he's hatching a plan.

"I was thinking more of the local library," he said.

"What if somebody spots us there?"

"We'll have to take that chance."

"Let's say it is him, Frank—then what?"

"Hmmm . . ."

Frank massaged his eyes with his palms for a minute, then came up with an idea. "He goes up in his plane at night, right? What if we stow away and go with him?"

A big smile spread over my face at the thought. *Beautiful.* We catch him in the act—a couple of ghosts come back to life!

"Okay then," Frank said, obviously noting my approval. "Compromise: We'll do both: Internet search and stow away."

"Deal."

We finished eating and headed over to the library. It was just across the street from city hall, so we had to be careful. There was no sign of Bump Rankowski, thank goodness, but those two guys who jumped us on the beach might have been around somewhere.

We didn't know what they looked like, but they must have known our faces.

Of course they wouldn't be looking for us, because they thought we were dead.

First time death was in our favor.

Inside, we went right over to a bank of computers, well-hidden from general view behind a row of bookshelves. Frank sat down and did a search for Bump Rankowski.

A bunch of stuff came up—about his businesses, his first mayoral campaign, his winning a flying contest. . . .

"He's running for reelection in the fall," Frank pointed out.

"So?"

"So, if he wants to get reelected—and he sure seems to like the job—he might be tempted to start a tourist 'gold rush,' right?"

"Totally. I'm convinced, Frank. It's him. Let's get out of here and take care of business."

"Wait a second. Cool your jets, Joe. There's no proof in here—not enough to go on."

"But Frank—"

"We've got to have more than this," he insisted.

Then it hit me.

"Hey, remember he said Bump wasn't always his name?"

"Right! Now what was it . . . ? Adam? Something with an A . . ."

I suddenly remembered. "Arnold!"

"That's it!"

Frank keyed in Arnold Rankowski, and a moment later we hit the jackpot. There was an article from the *Sea Bright Gazette,* dated 1984, all about the arrest of one Arnold Rankowski on charges of petty thievery—from a jewelry store!

"Paydirt!" Frank said, and printed out the article.

There were more, too—our boy Arnold had three more minor offenses to his name.

No wonder he'd changed it!

"So here's our case," Frank said, gathering all the printouts together. "Three felony arrests along with two misdemeanors. Suspended sentence for the first felony, community service for the second, three months in Rahway State Prison for the third. Nothing since 1985."

"How did he ever become mayor?" I said. "Wouldn't somebody have dragged out his past during the campaign and used it against him?"

Frank did some more searching.

"Hang on," he finally said. "November 7, 1992. Front page of the *Ocean Point Gazette*: 'Rankowski Wins in Squeaker.'" He scrolled down and continued reading: "'Arnold "Bump" Rankowski was elected mayor yesterday with 52 percent of the votes counted. Steve Lyons conceded defeat at 10 P.M. Most observers agreed that Rankowski's heroic efforts last week in spotting and putting out a potentially devastating fire at the amusement pier helped erase the negative effects of his somewhat shady past.'"

"I'll bet he set that fire himself," I said.

"I wouldn't put it past him," Frank agreed. "Bump seems to have a way of manipulating events to suit himself."

"I'll bet he robbed those three jewelry stores, Frank," I said. "He figured he'd drop the loot on the beach, create a gold rush, and get reelected by a landslide!"

"And Joe, think about this—as mayor, he could have waltzed into police headquarters at any time and pulled the codes for the jewelry stores' alarm systems off the police computer!"

"Huh?"

"Stores with alarm systems hooked in to police and fire headquarters have to provide them with the codes to disable the system."

"Ah, I get it," I said.

"I think we're getting a pretty clear picture of Bump Rankowski," Frank said as he got up.

"That slimeball. Let's not forget, he tried to have

us killed when he realized we were close to cracking the case!"

We had our man, all right. All we had to do now was catch him red-handed.

Tonight was the night—and I could hardly wait.

17.

Up in the Air

We called a cab to come get us at our hotel and bring us to the Ocean Point Airport. I took the precaution of calling one from Atlantic City. Sure, it was expensive, but there was no way we could be sure the local cab owners weren't FOB: Friends of Bump.

The airport closed at 11 P.M. I was fairly sure Bump wouldn't be doing his treasure dumping before then. Trudging through the terminal building with a big sack of jewelry would be pretty hard for anyone to miss.

Besides, it had been nearly 4 A.M. when Joe got smacked on the head by that bracelet. My bet was that Bump didn't show up till well after 2 A.M.

Joe and I waited in the darkness across the road from the terminal until everyone had left for the night, and most of the lights had been turned off. Then we ran across the road and hopped the chain-link fence that separated the terminal from the runway.

It was easy to find Bump's plane—those shark teeth and eyes stood out even in the semidarkness. You could even make out that the plane was bright red. It almost glowed in the moonlight.

We had to do this all in a hurry. At any moment a car passing by on the road might shine its headlights right at us—or an airport employee we hadn't accounted for might decide to check the planes out.

Anything could happen.

So we jogged over to Bump's pride and joy. The canopy was locked—no problem, though. I fished out my pocketknife and jimmied it. Sure, the destroyed lock might make Bump suspicious when he saw it, but if our plan worked, he'd be behind bars before he had a chance to notice.

We quietly raised the canopy and climbed inside. Only after we'd shut it behind us did we feel we could relax.

At least for now.

"Got the camera?" Joe asked.

I patted the pocket of my windbreaker. The cheap disposable camera ATAC had given us was there, ready and primed for action.

"Got the night scope? You found it after we got dug out, right?"

I took it out and gave it to Joe, and he started scanning the airport on the other side of the clear plastic canopy.

"What's the use of doing that?" I asked him. "We'll see the headlights when Bump parks his car."

"And what if someone drops him off down the road, and he walks the rest of the way and ends up taking us by surprise?"

I didn't think it was too likely, but I agreed that Joe had a point.

Still, as the hours wore on and there was no sign of Bump Rankowski, it started to get boring—and tiring.

We were still sleep-deprived, and we had to keep nudging one another to stay awake, especially once it got past 2 A.M.

When 4 A.M. came and went, Joe began to get really antsy. "He's not coming. It's not him. We've got this all wrong, Frank."

"What?"

"It's somebody else—one of our other suspects. That lifeguard, Chucky Whatzizname. Or the tattoo guy, Ricardo. Or one of the Russian guys."

"Joe . . ."

"I don't want to waste our time waiting for a guy who's not coming."

"Okay, wait a minute," I said. "First, I'll remind you that you're the one who was so convinced it was Bump, from the minute you got hit with that bracelet. Second, someone's dropping jewelry out of a plane. Bump has a plane—in fact, he owns a fleet of them. He's got motive, opportunity, and means."

"All right, but now I think I was wrong. He's still not here, right? What time is it?"

"Five minutes later than the last time you asked."

"Come on, wise guy. What time?"

"Four ten."

"And still no Bump. I rest my case."

Wouldn't you know it, just then a pair of headlights came into view down the road, swinging right toward the airport.

When the car pulled into the lot and stopped, it was time to hunker down and get ready. We settled ourselves behind the rear seats of the plane, completely hidden from view.

The canopy opened, and Bump's sizeable figure appeared in silhouette. I could hear him breathing hard as he settled himself into the pilot's seat and closed the canopy over his head. "That's funny," he mumbled. "Coulda sworn I locked it. . . . Oh, well."

Joe and I looked at each other. We were trying hard not to make a sound. We couldn't see Bump, but we could hear him going through his checklist, humming a happy little tune as he went.

That scum, I thought. *He thinks he's killed a couple of kids, and that makes him want to burst into song!*

I knew Joe felt like jumping him then and there, so I put my hand on his arm, reminding him that we had to wait until we had the evidence we needed.

Bump got the engine going and nosed the Cessna onto the runway. Soon we were airborne—but not without a struggle. With me and Joe on board, the plane was about 300 pounds heavier than Bump realized, and he had to give it a bit more lift than he thought.

"What the—?" I heard him grunt. "What's wrong with this thing?"

After a minute, he'd figured out how to get us

up to a safe altitude. He circled around, no doubt heading for the beach.

Two minutes later we heard the pilot's side canopy window open. Then there was the jingling of the sack of jewels he was carrying with him.

"Now!" Joe mouthed.

I sprang up, camera in hand, and fired off three pictures before Bump knew what hit him.

"What the—? HEY!"

He dropped the bag and tried to hide his face. The plane yawed and pitched crazily, and Bump had to grab the controls—which kept him from going after us.

"Who's that?" he shouted. "Who's that back there?"

But we weren't back there any more. Leapfrogging the seats, we were now right behind him.

"You!" he gasped.

"Sorry we're not dead," Joe said.

With that, he grabbed Bump's left arm, twisting it behind his back. Bump's right hand came off the controls, and I grabbed it—but only until his foot lashed out and caught me in the head.

I let go, reeling backward, and the plane did a full, sickening rollover. Joe almost wound up going out the open window.

And Bump had time to recover his wits.

He backed into Joe, trying to force him out the window, while flailing at me with his feet.

The plane was still rolling over, and it was all I could do to steady myself. Finally I twisted around and sat on Bump's outstretched legs.

My back was toward him, but now I could grab the throttle and try to steady the plane. I mean, there was no point in catching Bump if we all wound up dead in a plane crash, was there?

Maybe we should have thought this through a little better.

But then, this was the fun part.

Joe was dangling out the window, but Bump was too busy choking me to push him the rest of the way out.

I elbowed Bump in the ribs until he let go, then swung back around, dodging a punch on the way.

Joe had managed to fall back into the plane, and Bump was climbing over the seats, headed for the rear. I kept hold of the throttle while Joe faced him down.

"It's two against one, Mayor," Joe said, balling his fists and slowly closing in for the finish. "I think you should give up."

Bump reached down behind the backseat—right

where we'd been crouching down in the dark—
and drew out a big, fat pistol.

"Maybe this evens things up," he said, pointing
it right at Joe's face.

18.

Defying Gravity

It was a little too dark, and I was a little too distracted, to tell exactly what kind of pistol was staring me down. Believe me when I tell you, though, that it was plenty big enough to blow my head off.

Especially from three feet away, which is where Bump was standing.

Frank was busy with the controls, but if he didn't do something fast, it wouldn't matter if we crashed or not.

But what was he supposed to do? If he made a move, it was the big bang, and *good-bye, Joe Hardy!*

"So," Frank said to Bump, "you're going to shoot us?"

154

"Only if I have to," Bump answered, wiping the blood off his mouth. "I'd rather not mess up my plane. I'd much prefer it if you boys would jump. You know, I thought you two had washed away with the tide."

"We got lucky," I said.

Bump laughed. "Right. Well, I guess your luck has just run out." He cocked the gun. "Now, are you gonna make me shoot you? Or are you gonna cooperate?"

We didn't answer. I was pinned down and couldn't risk moving, and Frank was steering the plane.

"Out that window will do," Bump said, pointing to it with one hand while the other held the gun right at me.

"You first," he said to Frank.

I saw Frank's eyes shift, and I knew what he was thinking. A quick jerk on the throttle, and maybe it would throw Bump off balance enough for us to overpower him.

But there was no guarantee of success. And if he messed up, I was dead.

"And no funny business," Bump said quickly, "or your brother gets a big fat bullet in the head."

Obviously, he'd read Frank's mind, same as I had.

"Slowly, now," Bump told him. "Not one false move. Hands off the controls."

Frank did as he was told. He gave me a long look, then climbed out the window. Headfirst.

Nice acting, bro. Nice.

I could see him clinging to the wing. The plane, dragged by his weight, started to bank to the left.

"Now you," Bump said to me. "Turn around and start moving."

I followed Frank out the window, and I didn't try jumping Bump. I didn't know how we were going to get out of this alive. All I knew was, I trusted my brother and his convoluted brain. I had faith that Frank, as always, had a plan.

"So long, boys!" Bump yelled before closing the window behind us. He grabbed the controls, but he was still fighting our weight, which was now dragging the plane to one side.

"Quick!" Frank yelled to me. "We've got to get to the center. Climb on top of the fuselage."

I followed his instructions. It was hard to hold on—the plane had to be going eighty miles an hour, and we were at least a thousand feet up.

The wind was so powerful it pushed me back along the top of the plane. I slid until I hit the tail—which was right between my legs.

OW!!

I winced in pain. Could it be worse?

At least I wasn't going to fall off from this position. I guess.

Now I saw Frank, sliding back toward me. His right foot hit me square in the head. Right into my black eyes.

OW!!

Yeah. It could be worse.

At least now we were both firmly attached to the plane, with good footholds and handholds.

Just in time, too, because Bump had realized we were there and was trying his best to shake us off.

He was doing rollovers.

We held on with sheer muscle power, fighting gravity, until Bump had to right the plane or risk crashing.

In fact, now that Frank and I were firmly attached to the tail section, the whole plane was dragging—so much so that it might tip upward and stall out at any moment.

Frank looked back at me.

"What do we do now?" I asked him.

"Look behind you!" he yelled.

I did—and there, trailing behind us, was a big,

long banner. EAT AT RON'S LOBSTER SHACK, it said.

"How did that get there?" I shouted.

"One of us must have hit the release button by accident! Joe—it's our way out of this!"

"What?"

"Climb out on the banner!"

"Are you crazy?"

"We'll make it into a parachute!"

"A parachute?"

"Aunt Trudy, Joe! Remember? Bottom left corner, top right corner . . ."

Now I saw what he was getting at.

It was a long shot, all right. But it just might work.

I waited for a moment when Bump wasn't trying to shake us off. Then I eased myself around the tail, grabbed onto the banner, and swung myself off the plane. Gradually, little by little, hand over hand, I let myself out toward the far end, while Frank followed behind me.

I watched as he took out his pocketknife and flipped it open. "Ready?" he called to me.

I nodded.

"Grab your two corners!" he shouted. "And hold on!"

He cut the cord holding the banner to the plane, and with a sudden snap, we were floating free.

Plummeting free is more like it, really.

I spread my hands wide, trying to keep the banner as open as possible.

The tug on my arms was tremendous. Good thing I'd worked out before we left.

Across from me, Frank was grimacing as he held his corners. The veins in his neck looked like they were going to pop out.

The ocean was getting closer by the second. I could see it in the dawn's early light. We were right over the shore and drifting toward the beach. If we hit the sand at this speed, we were goners.

I looked up for a second, and I saw Bump's plane spinning downward, out of control. The shock when we'd cut our weight loose must have made him stall out!

As we got closer to a deadly crash-landing, I stared at the beach below us. I was more terrified than I'd ever been in my life.

Was this it? Were we really going to die like this?

My whole life flashed before my eyes in a second. Dad, Mom, Aunt Trudy, all my friends . . . and most of all, Frank, who was going through the same thing, I'm sure.

BOOM!!

I heard the explosion—Bump and his plane

hitting the water at 100 miles an hour. *Well, he got what he deserved,* I thought.

Small satisfaction, though. In about five seconds, we'd be as dead as he was.

I closed my eyes and braced for impact. . . .

KATHUNK!!!

Am I dead?

My mouth was full of sand. So were my eyes. They stung.

I hurt all over.

But . . . if everything hurt, I couldn't be dead, right?

"Joe, are you okay?" It was Frank's voice.

He was alive too!

I spat a wad of sand out of my mouth. I still seemed to have all my teeth. This was good.

I tried to open my eyes. It took a while to get the sand out of them and actually see anything.

Finally, I saw Frank standing over me, covered with sand—but very much alive.

I stood up—slowly, carefully—and stared at the mound of soft sand that had saved both me and Frank from certain death. . . .

It was the Taj Mahal. Carl Jardine's amazing sand sculpture!

Funny.

Perfect.

His masterpiece was totaled, all right—but *we* were still whole. Which proves one thing: It's lucky to be smart, but it's even smarter to be lucky.

19.

There's No Place Like Home

We paid a big chunk of money to get driven back to Bayport by limo. Both Joe and I were way too sore to drive, and neither of us wanted to hop in a plane again anytime soon.

We'd spent the whole day being checked over at the Ocean Point Community Hospital (lots of bruises, but amazingly, no broken bones—thanks to Aunt Trudy and her Code of Perfect Sheet-Folding).

The police didn't believe our story at first, but when they found some of the stolen loot in the desk drawer of Bump's office at city hall, they decided to let us go.

We could have hung around for a real vacation, but Ocean Point was the last place we wanted to be right then. Both of us felt like Dorothy at the end of *The Wizard of Oz*: "There's no place like home."

We rolled up in front of our house and slowly, painfully, got out of the limo.

Mom and Aunt Trudy were out front, weeding the flower garden. Playback was perched on Trudy's shoulder, as usual.

"What the—?" Mom gasped when she caught sight of us.

I knew we were in for it.

"What have you boys been up to *this* time?" Aunt Trudy asked. "Look at them, Laura—they're black and blue all over. You boys have been getting into fights again, haven't you? Don't deny it!"

"Now, Trudy," said good old Mom, "I'm sure if the boys were fighting, it's only because they were provoked."

"Oh, *right*," said Trudy. "'They're good boys, your honor!' *Hmph!*"

"Now, Trudy," Mom said, "let's not jump to conclusions. I'm sure Frank and Joe can explain everything. Let's go inside and have some lemonade, and they can tell us all about their adventures on the Shore."

Lemonade? Yes, please.

Between the driveway and the kitchen, I was sure I could come up with something to tell them.

Something that wasn't the truth, but that would sound enough like it to satisfy them.

"Liar, liar, pants on fire!" Playback squawked, staring straight at me.

I put a hand on Joe's arm before he could go for the parrot.

"By the way," Aunt Trudy said as we crossed the living room, "those sheets you folded last Saturday? All wrong. I had to do them over again—corners weren't lined up at all! When are you boys *ever* going to learn?"

"Now, Trudy," Mom said, "the boys are all bruised and banged up. Let's not pester them about the sheets. After all, perfectly folded sheets aren't a matter of life and death."

Ah, but how wrong she was!

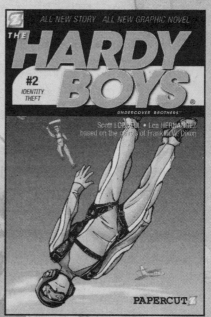

Exciting fiction from three-time Newbery Honor author Gary Paulsen

Aladdin Paperbacks and Simon Pulse
Simon & Schuster Children's Publishing
www.SimonSays.com

PENDRAGON

Bobby Pendragon is a seemingly normal fourteen-year-old boy. He has a family, a home, and a possible new girlfriend. But something happens to Bobby that changes his life forever.

HE IS CHOSEN TO DETERMINE THE COURSE OF HUMAN EXISTENCE.

Pulled away from the comfort of his family and suburban home, Bobby is launched into the middle of an immense, interdimensional conflict involving racial tensions, threatened ecosystems, and more. It's a journey of danger and discovery for Bobby, and his success or failure will do nothing less than determine the fate of the world. . . .

PENDRAGON

by D. J. MacHale

Book One: The Merchant of Death
Book Two: The Lost City of Faar
Book Three: The Never War
Book Four: The Reality Bug
Book Five: Black Water

Coming Soon: Book Six: The Rivers of Zadaa

From Aladdin Paperbacks • Published by Simon & Schuster